"I believe this samb... on it."

"No more shoptalk," she said when he set his hands on her waist and followed her to the dance floor. "But neck nuzzling is definitely allowed."

For a moment, as they passed the line of French doors, she heard the wind raging outside. Then it was all music and the magic of the moment. And Tal.

He was hot, and dazzling her with his aura. The sexy, sensual essence that was and always had been uniquely Tal. She was losing herself in it, until he spoke.

"This isn't why I came tonight, Maya," he said against her hair. "I don't want to hurt you." Lowering his head, he slid his tongue over her ear. "You're not making this any easier."

"You couldn't hurt me if you wanted to, Tal."

"Consider yourself warned," he murmured against her throat before he kissed her.

JENNA RYAN

KISSING *the* KEY WITNESS

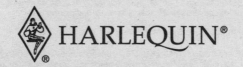

HARLEQUIN®

TORONTO • NEW YORK • LONDON
AMSTERDAM • PARIS • SYDNEY • HAMBURG
STOCKHOLM • ATHENS • TOKYO • MILAN • MADRID
PRAGUE • WARSAW • BUDAPEST • AUCKLAND

Merlyn;
You were the love and the joy of our lives.
On to the next big adventure.
Have fun, sweetheart…

Recycling programs
for this product may
not exist in your area.

ISBN-13: 978-0-373-69402-0
ISBN-10:   0-373-69402-4

KISSING THE KEY WITNESS

ABOUT THE AUTHOR

Jenna Ryan loves creating dark-haired heroes, heroines with strength and good murder mysteries. Ever since she was young, she has had an extremely active imagination. She considered various careers over the years and dabbled in several of them, until the day her sister Kathy suggested she put her imagination to work and write a book. She enjoys working with intriguing characters and feels she is at her best writing romantic suspense. When people ask her how she writes, she tells them by instinct. Clearly it's worked, since she's received numerous awards from *Romantic Times BOOKreviews*. She lives in Canada and travels as much as she can when she's not writing.

Books by Jenna Ryan

CAST OF CHARACTERS

Maya Santino—An E.R. doctor, she was the last person her ex spoke to before he died.

Stephen Talbot (Tal)—Miami Homicide lieutenant, he must protect Maya from the people who want to kill her.

Gene 'Quick Draw' McGraw—How far will the Fraud cop go for a promotion to Homicide?

Don Drake—The Homicide captain is living better than he should.

Nate Hammond—The retired Fraud captain pursued but never caught his notorious nemesis.

Jamie Hazell—The E.R. nurse has serious financial problems.

Orlando Perine—The powerful corporate mogul has cops on his payroll and a very vindictive nature.

Falcom—He turned on his powerful boss. Now, he is desperate to get back the information he sold to the police.

Adam Tyler—Maya's ex-husband hid important information right before he died.

Prologue

August in Miami.

Even in the dead of night, the air felt heavy. Prickles, like spiky fingernails, danced along fraud detective Adam Tyler's spine. He smelled more than fetid air outside the waterfront warehouse. Anticipation carried its own scent, and he'd been breathing it since late afternoon.

Too bad his captain had gone deep-sea fishing for the weekend, unplugged and incommunicado until Sunday night. But no sweat. Adam had been a detective since before his ill-fated marriage seven years ago. He could sit on anything, big or small, for a couple of days.

"Yeah, right." He grinned as he pulled the parking brake on his prized 1967 Shelby Mustang. "And pink elephants really do exist."

He glanced at his watch before heading to one of the small bay doors. He'd met snitches here countless times over the years. The Cuban-born owners knew that but said nothing, because—big surprise—they didn't want the contents of their shipping crates examined by anyone calling himself a cop.

The prickles continued to tap-dance across his skin,

Adam gave his eyes a few seconds to adjust, then made his way to the storage unit's crowded center.

It smelled worse in here than outside. Tiny claws scrabbled on concrete as he squeezed between the towering crates. Catching a movement ahead, he let the grin return. His informant was acting more like the rodents around him than the bird of prey whose code name he'd adopted. The man's head shot up as Adam's holster scraped across the face of a crate marked Bananas.

"Only me," he said when Falcon's hand crawled inside his hoodie. "For the record, I was off duty and halfway across the city when you called."

"I want it back."

Adam resisted the urge to laugh. Not only had his snitch been pacing like a jittery rat, but in the bad light he actually resembled one. A cartoon version, with popping eyes, long fingers and feet comically elongated by deep patches of black.

He stuffed his hands in his pockets. "Sorry, pal, but it's done. I've got my evidence. You've got your immunity. Fair deal all around."

"I've changed my mind. I don't want to turn him in."

Adam leaned on one of the towers. "Uh, refresh my memory. Who came to whom, begging for help?"

Falcon spoke through clenched teeth. "I had my reasons back then. Situation's changed. I want it back."

"Not an option." Adam reached for his backup weapon. "And if you're thinking about shooting me for it, you'll be wasting good bullets. I've already—"

"Your captain's gone fishing," Falcon blurted, then offered a cynical smile. "I've got my sources, too, Tyler. You haven't turned it over yet. Can't until Monday. Means my boss'll be free to kill me for another sixty hours. Even then I won't be safe. I'm not the only person on his payroll."

"Just the most cowardly." Adam shrugged. "Or maybe the most desperate."

"Do you know what he's capable of?"

"I've seen his work."

Falcon made a frantic flapping motion. "He's got, like, elephant ears."

"Well, I've got, like, elephant feet, and one of them's about to boot you in your canary yellow ass. He won't—"

"He will."

"Falcon, even Orlando Perine wouldn't—"

His informant surged forward, teeth bared. "Talk about asses. I'm telling you, Tyler, he'll yawn while he's pulling the trigger. That's how big a deal murder is to him. We're talking ice water for blood. Reptilian brain. No emotion. Okay, I was desperate to get out, get away, so I did something stupid. But he found out. He knows someone's turned. Doesn't know who. Only that one of his people sold him out. Or is about to. Bottom line? It's not worth the risk. I'd rather go to prison and live than die the way he'll kill me if he finds out what I've done."

Adam pushed off the tower of crates. "Have you been taking drama lessons as well as drugs? Gear down and breathe, okay? No one's going to die. And no one but me is ever going to know—"

A sudden sharp pain in his shoulder, followed by another to the left of his spinal column, brought him up short. Blinking, he looked down at the front of his shirt. Twin blotches of red spread quickly across the fabric.

"Oh, hell…"

His vision wavered. He heard Falcon swear; saw him jump sideways and vanish behind a crate.

The prickles on his spine turned to claws that scratched so deeply, they scored his lungs. His chest heated and filled. His mind began to fade.

"Guess I was wrong," he murmured. "Looks like someone's going to die, after all."

The black took over as he pitched face-forward onto the warehouse floor.

Chapter One

"Maya, wait!"

So close, Maya Santino reflected, with a sigh. She'd actually made it to the staff exit this time.

A lanky E.R. nurse swooped in from the side. "Nice try, Doc, but it's a no go." Spotting Maya's earbuds, she cupped a hand to her mouth. "I said, we need you, Dr. S."

"Yes, I gathered that, Jamie." She pulled out the earbuds and stuffed the iPod into her oversize bag. "What's the problem?"

"McVey's here."

Although she wanted to resist, Maya let her friend and colleague propel her back along the corridor. "You do know I was coming off a ten-hour shift even before that last two-hour meeting, right?"

"Is it my fault the man won't see anyone but you?" Jamie Hazell continued to push her forward. "Admissions says his hand's wrapped in a filthy towel, but he flat out refuses to go to the clinic. Says it's you or no one. There's Lysol at the desk if you want it."

Maya grinned. "My uncle raises chickens in South America. Spend a weekend on his farm, then talk to me about McVey." A brow went up. "Treatment room four?"

"As far from the madding crowd as possible."

"There's a madding crowd?"

Jamie swept a hand in front of her as they rounded the corner. "You decide."

From Maya's perspective, it was only mild mayhem. She'd seen much worse during her three-year tenure at Miami's Eden Bay Hospital. Once, the sea of gurneys had been so deep, she'd been forced to climb over one to reach another.

Of course, they'd been smack in the middle of the hurricane season then. Storm after storm had pelted the southern coast. There'd been home and highway accidents, tramplings and assaults. Scores of buildings had been damaged. Maya's roof had taken two beatings from uprooted trees. Her car had gotten it from a toppled streetlamp.

Reaching out, she straightened her friend's name badge. "Cheer up, Nurse Hazell. You're transferring out of the E.R., remember? Thirty days and counting."

"Unless Dr. Driscoll changes his mind. It's happened before. Enjoy your patient."

Five minutes later, her earbuds replaced by a stethoscope around the collar of her lab coat, Maya pushed through the treatment-room door.

McVey—it was the only name he used—sat on a table. His thin shoulders were hunched, and his back was bowed. The thought struck, as it often did, that he seemed familiar in some way. Then, poof, the thought vanished, and he was just McVey again, a man currently in a great deal of pain.

He supported his injured left hand with a grimy right.

He might not live on the street, but Maya suspected the odd jobs he did at a low-income apartment complex didn't keep him far from it.

"Okay." Using her two index fingers, she indicated the bloody towel. "What's the story?"

"Got slammed in a furnace door. Rusty metal, sharp edges. Tore the skin when I jerked free. Uh, is Witch—sorry, Nurse Hazell working tonight?"

"I'm afraid so."

Maya watched his face as she unwrapped the towel. He kept his eyes averted. Meant he was lying about something, though she figured the rusty-metal part was probably true enough.

"Any point asking if you've had a tetanus shot over the past decade?"

He almost smiled, but still didn't meet her eyes. "Any point trying to fake you out?"

"Not much." It was a deep gash that would require several stitches. "Why me?"

Another near smile. "Because you're pretty?"

"Other doctors are prettier."

"But only you remind me of Sabrina."

"Excuse me?"

"The movie, remember? Audrey Hepburn was the title character. She grew up and was transformed, like you've done since you came here as a resident."

"Have I known you that long? Huh, blink and the years fly by."

A grim-faced Jamie came into the room. She sorted through the instrument tray while Maya finished her examination.

McVey's eyes narrowed. "You're not gonna spray me again, are you, Nurse?"

"I'd like to do more than spray you," Jamie retorted, with an expression that made Maya's lips twitch.

"Careful," she warned when McVey opened his mouth. "Remember, Nurse Hazell administers the local."

He pressed his lips together for the duration, even took the tetanus shot without a whimper. But then she suspected he was accustomed to injections and, if the alcohol on his breath was any indication, not in quite as much pain as he could be.

"Okay. Done." She snapped off her latex gloves. "Grab a doughnut on your way out."

The door cracked open, and an intern's head appeared. "Sorry to interrupt, Doctor, but there's been a pileup on the interstate. Twenty, maybe thirty cars. Several injuries, and we're the closest E.R."

"We're also the most understaffed," Jamie called after him. "Crap. Why's it always us?"

"Fate or proximity to the freeway. Take your pick." Maya started for the door. "Keep that hand as clean as you can, McVey. Come back Monday, before I go off shift, and I'll look at it."

Her attention shifted instantly at the sound of sirens wailing. She joined the line of attendants jogging toward the entrance.

It was going to be a very long night.

EVERYTHING AROUND HIM had gone gray and blurry, even with his eyes open. Sort of open, Adam amended, inasmuch as he could think with the light that kept tugging at him. Beautiful light, silvery and soft. It had siren qualities, but he resisted the lure.

He sensed movement, saw the gray haze alter. Ugly

streaks of red slashed it apart. Noise, like shrieking daggers, jabbed into his brain. Hands clutched his shoulders and shook him.

"Don't die," Falcon pleaded from above. "I need that information back."

Adam would have laughed if an anvil hadn't been sitting on his chest.

"I have to go." The snitch's voice faded. "Someone'll help you. I'll come back when you're better. I don't think he saw me in the warehouse. I think you blocked his view...."

Probably true, Adam thought fuzzily. Man, this had definitely not been his night.

The darkness thickened, grew hotter, stickier. He couldn't swallow, could no longer think. Faces flashed inside the red. His ex-wife's, his old friend's, his new enemy's.

Voices shouted indistinct words. The hands on his shoulders fell away. He heard Falcon swear, then a more familiar voice.

"Adam?"

Startled but not panicky. Female.

"Maya?"

She leaned over, and he saw her face. Exotic features, dark hair, incredible eyes. Bluer than a tropical lagoon.

"Screwed up," he murmured. "Made you hate me."

"I don't hate you."

Maybe not, but she was waking the pain anyway.

The light around him intensified. He was breathing fire now. He felt her hands on him and groped until he caught her wrist. "Stop," he croaked. "Listen."

"Adam, I can't help you if—"

"I'm dead, Maya. I know it, and so do you. Do this for me, please."

"Do what?"

He squeezed. "Take care of things. Made a will last year. Straightforward. Money, investments—they're my sister's. Condo's yours. Go through it and— Ahh!" Pain sheared from chest to brain. He had to talk through his teeth. "Don't let my brother have the Mustang... Crash addict. Give my sweet baby to Tal." He fumbled two sets of keys from his pocket. "Condo keys, car keys. Promise."

"Yes, okay, I promise. Now let me help...."

"There's more. Stuff, official stuff. Hid it. Don't trust anyone, anywhere. Huge mistake. Big fish, small pond. S'all I can say. Tell Tal to finish the deal."

The light flared. It seemed to explode like a starburst that went from a bang to a fizzle.

"Sorry, babe." He rattled out a breath. "I'll tell your mom you're good."

"Adam?" Now she shook him. "Adam!"

The last thing he saw was her face. Then the sparkles died, and there was nothing.

"Dr. Santino?" A nurse with red curls and acne touched her sleeve as she stared at her ex-husband's face. "A lower body trauma's just come in. Female. Six months pregnant."

Through the buzz of shock in her head, Maya caught the last part of the nurse's statement. She shook off what she could and refocused. "Where?"

"Over there." The young nurse—Cassie? Callie?—pointed. She looked down, then hesitantly up. "Can I, uh, do anything for you?"

"No. Thanks, but no." With a hand that wanted to

shake, Maya closed Adam's eyes. She regarded the paramedic who'd helped her lift him from the ground to the gurney. "Take him inside. I'll be right there."

"Got a bleeder over here," another nurse called.

The words jarred. "Thirty seconds," Maya told the redhead. "Get Jamie to take the bleeder."

Turning away, she pressed two fingers to her temples. She needed to settle herself, to absorb what had just happened.

Adam had always been a risk taker. She'd loved him once, hated him briefly, then figured to hell with it and dealt with her mistakes. With her mistakes.

They'd been strangers, for the most part, after the divorce. He'd transferred to Orlando, but returned to Miami sixteen months ago, because his roots were here, he'd said.

She understood roots. Hers were mostly here, too. In any case, she hadn't hated him by then.

"Doctor Santino?"

Her thirty seconds were up. Adam was dead. She couldn't make him undead by standing outside the emergency room, ignoring the injured while a host of memories swamped her.

"I'm really sorry, Adam." Head tipped back, she spoke to the night sky. Then shut down and fixed her attention on the living.

"ARE YOU AWAKE, TAL?" DON Drake's voice hacked rudely into Stephen Talbot's dream.

"Go away," Tal said into the phone. "I'm still working the Demorno case."

"You're done enough to be back in Miami, so listen up. I got a call from Lieutenant Morse in fraud."

Tal tried to prop his eyes open. When that failed, he rolled onto his back and let the watery light outside play against his lids. "You've got about ten seconds before my brain shuts down. This is the first time I've seen a bed in three days."

"Tyler's dead," his captain growled.

That worked. He went up on one elbow. "Adam Tyler?"

"You got it. He was shot late tonight, died in the E.R."

Tal swung his feet to the floor. "Eden Bay?"

"You're two for two. He went to his ex for help—or was taken there. Details are sketchy. McGraw's on his way over to firm up what he can, but since homicide and fraud are more or less cooperating on the Perine investigation, I want a rep there, too. Tyler was a cop, Tal. He was one of us. I know you're familiar with the case he was working on, even if you weren't directly involved. I want that shooter nailed. Tyler was your friend, so I'm thinking you'll want the same thing."

Tal's sleep-deprived mind resisted the attempt to shove it into line. When had he and Adam talked last? Seven, maybe eight days ago, and only briefly then. Adam had called him in Tampa.

"He said he had a line on Orlando Perine."

"Had a hook in the bastard's mouth, near as I can tell." Drake gave a grunt. "Grill McGraw, see what he knows, but don't count on him giving you straight answers. You know how the fraud boys are. Vultures over a rotting carcass."

Standing, Tal bulldozed the last of the grogginess from his brain. His old academy friend was dead. He'd died at Eden Bay Hospital. Adam's ex-wife worked at Eden Bay. Had she seen him, spoken to him? Hell, had she watched him die?

With the light off and the phone wedged between his shoulder and ear, he located his jeans. "Adam was working with an informant last week," he said. "Some guy who wanted out. Didn't get a name."

"He didn't, or you didn't?"

"Both. He called the guy Falcon."

Dragging a T-shirt over his head, Tal searched for boots, sneakers, shoes—anything wearable. He found a pair of black hikers on the closet floor and, holding his keys in his mouth, laced them on.

"You know Tyler's ex, don't you?" the captain asked.

Tal grabbed a jacket. "We've met."

"Use it. Tyler was a good cop, and homicide's our business. We call the shots. Fraud's on the sidelines here. Make sure McGraw understands that."

Tal really didn't care what McGraw understood. Adam had been his friend. Whether officially or unofficially, this was his case now.

"Heading out," he said and tossed the handset aside.

Adam Tyler was dead. And the man responsible was going to pay.

"YOU CAN'T OUTRUN THE TRUTH, Ms. Santino. Someone shot your ex-husband. Someone who works for Orlando Perine, aka the slimiest scumbag in the Sunshine State."

Gene McGraw enunciated the last part of his statement as if speaking to a five-year-old child. Not the best approach, in Maya's opinion, but then if the rumors she'd heard about him had any merit, he wasn't the most tactful cop in the fraud division. He certainly wasn't the most incisive.

Three hours had passed since the first ambulance had pulled in. She'd lost count of how many patients she'd treated—which was just as well, since counting meant thinking, and thinking would lead her straight to Adam. Not that she could avoid that destination indefinitely. Detective McGraw was dragging her there despite the crush of activity around them.

Bumping him back, Maya palpated the ribs of a man groaning on a gurney outside an overflowing treatment room.

"Ms. Santino…"

She turned from the patient. "You don't seem to be getting it, Detective McGraw. I haven't got time for a cross-examination right now. Although it continues to escape your notice, we're a bit busy here."

"So the fact that your ex-husband's been murdered doesn't mean diddly to you?" He hitched a testy shoulder as a pair of paramedics elbowed past.

Appearance-wise, McGraw reminded Maya of a shaggy blond Columbo. In terms of attitude, however, the word *caveman* sprang to mind. Or perhaps more aptly, her cousin Diego, who she swore was a throwback to one of her mother's nastier Andalusian ancestors.

"Believe me, Detective, I'd give a great deal to be able to reverse time and bring Adam back, but I can't do that, and unless you know some secret science, neither can you. What I *can* do is help the people in the here and now. Once the last patient is treated, I'll be more than happy to answer any question you want to throw at me. Until then, the machine in the doctor's lounge has better coffee than the cafeteria. It's also free."

Tipping her lips into a quick smile, she sidestepped his arm and was out of range before he could object.

"Guess you told him, huh?"

Maya had her palm on the next treatment-room door

when another man's voice reached her. She turned to meet Stephen Talbot's cool gray eyes. "I'm kinda busy here, Tal. Questions will have to wait."

"What about emotions?"

"Same answer." Frustration rose, coupled with something she knew better than to pinpoint. "Don't push, okay? I might bite, and that's not how I want to react. Adam's gone. I'm making myself accept the truth, but I can't—I won't—let down someone whose life I might be able to save because of it. Any chance of any cop in Miami grasping that concept tonight?"

Tal raised his hands. "Message received, Dr. Santino. I'll wait in the lounge."

She tried very hard not to notice how tall he was or how incredibly, well, male, she supposed. How sexy. It felt wrong to be having thoughts like that. It definitely seemed inappropriate.

"Dr. Santino!"

With her eyes still on Tal, Maya pushed the door. "I'm here, Jamie. I've got a dozen more patients to see, Lieutenant, and that number doesn't include any new arrivals. You could be waiting for quite some time."

He ignored the stream of people rushing past. "Better waiting than lying on one of your tables. Do what you have to, Maya. I'll handle McGraw."

Great, she reflected, pushing through the door. Except that McGraw wasn't the problem.

THE MAN CALLING HIMSELF Falcon crouched under a palm tree behind a lilac bush and watched time crawl by. He was afraid to leave his hiding place, terrified that Adam Tyler hadn't blocked the shooter's view, after all.

But no, he had to believe he was still a man of

mystery in his boss's eyes. A wanted, hunted man, but still an unknown commodity.

What would the big man do now? Obvious answer, he'd go for the last person Tyler had spoken to. The doctor who just happened to be his ex-wife. Yeah, that's what he'd do, all right. And if Tyler had talked, if he'd told her...

Falcon began to hyperventilate. The woman wasn't a cop, wasn't trained. A little pain, and she'd crack, like the fatal egg he'd laid today.

He had to run, get away. Let Tyler's ex die. Beautiful she might be, but beauty wouldn't help her, couldn't save her.

Giddy laughter swelled as he regarded the silhouette of the hospital before him. The woman was as dead as her ex-husband.

She just didn't know it yet.

Chapter Two

"Well, well. If it isn't Drake's go-to guy, hanging out in the E.R. at one of Miami's top three hospitals. Wish I thought you were here because you'd been shot. However, since you appear to be walking upright, looks like I'm out of luck."

Tal didn't bother to turn or even look up as Gene McGraw strode into the lounge. He wouldn't have made such a blustery entrance if there'd been other people around, but for the moment they were alone.

McGraw came to stand so close that his chest almost bumped Tal's arm. "You're looking a little unkempt, Lieutenant. Is this the appearance du jour of your homicide cronies up in Tampa?"

Raising a mug to his mouth, Tal turned. "You can't goad me, Gene. You don't matter enough at the moment."

"Oh, that's right. You and Tyler were pals, weren't you? Started out together on the street. Quick series of high-profile busts, and it was on to vice. Then a parting of the ways. Butch went to fraud, Sundance to homicide."

One thing McGraw seldom did was stir Tal's temper. God knew he had one. It simply couldn't be bothered squaring off with an overinflated jackass.

"Adam's dead, Gene. He was shot from behind with a nine-millimeter handgun. You worked with Tyler, so you can be here. But this is a homicide investigation."

Now McGraw did knock his thick chest into Tal's arm, just hard enough to slosh coffee onto the floor. He stuck a finger out for emphasis. "This, Lieutenant, is your captain yodeling his swan song and you vying for his job. Or maybe you want to bypass captain and shoot straight to the next level. Cop on a rocket to the gold stars." He flicked at the shaggy ends of Tal's hair. "Gonna have to tidy up some, though. Can't run a department looking like a back-alley gypsy."

Tal held his stare at close range for several seconds. "Still a homicide investigation, McGraw."

The detective's torso bulged. "You listen to me, you—'

"Oh, cool. A hormonal free-for-all. Can I watch?" Maya breezed into the room and went straight to the refrigerator.

Tal admired her savvy entrance—to say nothing of her other assets. Like the thick, coffee-colored hair she wore clipped back from the most striking face he'd ever seen. It never failed to amaze him just how jaw-dropping her features were. The woman very simply commanded attention. He should know. She'd commanded his for seven years.

He knew McGraw missed the glitter in her bluer than blue eyes when the burly detective planted intimidating hands on the counter and leaned toward her. "If you don't mind, Ms. Santori, I'll ask the questions. You only have to answer."

"It's Santino, and we did this dance earlier."

"Let's do it again. Be concise, and we'll be finished before you know it."

After a slight hesitation, her lips quirked. Not the best sign in Tal's opinion. "As you wish, Detective. I'll give you two minutes."

McGraw glanced at Tal, who shrugged and rested his butt on the table across the room. He opened with a gruff, "Did your husband—?"

"Ex-husband."

McGraw's features tightened. "Did your ex-husband," he repeated, "mention any names before he died?"

"Yes."

The detective glowered. "Well?"

"You said concise answers."

He pushed up to his full height of six feet four inches. "Whose name did he mention?"

"Tal's."

"Why was that?"

"Adam wanted him to have his Shelby Mustang."

Tal's eyes narrowed, but beyond that he didn't react.

"That's it?" McGraw demanded.

She smiled vaguely, as if at some private joke. "Adam and Tal rebuilt that car. Adam loved it. His brother's been involved in four traffic accidents over the past year. You don't leave treasure to a fool."

"No editorials necessary, Ms. Santino. Were there any other names?"

"He wanted his sister to take over his investments and for me to have his condo."

"Did he—?"

"Say anything unusual or extraordinary?" Anger was creeping in, but only to her voice. She kept those remarkable features schooled and her body, also remarkable, relaxed. "That would depend on your definition of the words. He said he'd tell my mother I was doing well. She died seven years ago." She capped her juice bottle, glanced at the wall clock. "*Tempus fugit,* Detective. Your two minutes are up." Reaching into the pocket of her lab coat, she produced a set of keys. "Yours," she said and tossed them to Tal.

He caught them left-handed and without taking his eyes off her.

McGraw reached the door first. "Would you recognize Orlando Perine if you saw him?"

Her brows went up. "As a matter of fact, I would."

"Did Tyler show you a picture?"

"No."

"Then how…?"

At a subtle head motion from Tal, she relented. "We had a board meeting last night to discuss the distribution of funds from a number of local businesses. The largest donation, over five hundred thousand dollars, came from Delgato Enterprises. If you don't know it, Delgato is the company president's mother's name. As I'm sure you do know, the company president is Orlando Perine."

"ARE YOU LEAVING?" JAMIE tried to respike her hair, which had wilted badly after six hours of nonstop action.

Maya tried—and failed—to focus her bleary eyes. "Yeah, definitely leaving. All the major traumas have been dealt with. Well, sort of dealt with."

Slumped against the locker-room wall, Jamie frowned. "Does the 'sort of' refer to your husband's death?"

"Ex-husband, and only partly. I'm still shell-shocked there. I think it has more to do with the police presence." Specifically, Tal's, but no way would she admit that out loud.

While Maya had half expected him to show tonight, after four years of not seeing him, the emotional punch had surprised her. Truthfully, it had blindsided her. Like watching Adam die...

"So, who was the cop?" Jamie gave her fingernails a casual inspection. "Not tall, dark and gorgeous—he's out of my league. I mean the big one who looked like a rumpled golden retriever."

"Gene McGraw. They call him Quick Draw, like the cartoon horse." She slipped off her work shoes and stepped into a pair of red heels. "This McGraw's more of a horse's ass, but I'm told he gets the job done."

"Is he married?"

"Are you serious?"

"Hey, twice divorced here, from bigger asses than your horse cop could ever be."

"You're a masochist, but I didn't see a wedding ring." Pulling on a light jacket over her jeans and tank, Maya closed her locker. "I want fresh air, a soft bed and no more cop questions. I figure if I'm lucky, I might get one of those things."

"Wait." Jamie caught her sleeve. "I want to tell you how sorry I am about Adam. I talked to him last spring, when he came in with a wounded suspect. I think he cared about you. A lot."

Because she knew her usually cynical friend meant well, Maya smiled. "Thanks. Don't let Driscoll bully you into double shifting."

She made it through the door this time, snagged an apple from the lounge and made her way along the maze of hallways to the staff exit.

Adam's face was in her mind. How could it not be? Then Tal's appeared over it, and she whooshed out a breath.

Did visualizing Tal above the man she'd married, divorced and watched die tonight make her a monster?

Did she want to answer that question?

"Not until my brain defogs," she said to the air.

Physicians were supposed to be compassionate, caring people. She had that covered. But what about selfless and forgiving? What about honest?

To block thought—and she desperately wanted to do that—she slipped her earbuds in and scanned her iPod for David Bowie.

Night had begun to fracture as dawn approached. Slivers of orange and red floated over a shimmering horizon.

They'd gotten married on the beach, she recalled. She'd let her mother arrange everything, from the rehearsal to the reception. She'd even let her set the larger-than-life guest list. She shouldn't have, but she'd known her mother was dying, and she'd wanted to indulge her in every possible way, right down to rushing into marriage with the wrong man.

At least her mother had wanted to see her married and happy, unlike her father, who'd ditched them both before Maya's fourth birthday in favor of— Well, twenty-six years later, that was still an open question. No one really knew what he'd wanted or where he'd gone.

Her uncles blamed his leaving on a pretty young accountant he'd met in Jamaica. Cousin Diego insisted he had a second family stashed away in Tennessee, but that was more likely Diego's own twisted fantasy. Her mother maintained he'd simply needed space.

The apple turned to mush in her mouth. Maya dropped the uneaten half in a trash can, breathed in the still-humid air and told herself it didn't matter why her father had taken off. It was the act that counted, and his leaving had hurt her mother far more than it had her.

Rooting through her shoulder bag, she located her keys. Tal would want to talk to her at some point. The thought came out of nowhere and brought a fatalistic "Damn" to her lips. Her avoidance layer was wearing extremely thin.

High above, palm fronds rustled. The shadows that lingered lengthened and shifted. The scent of verbena swirled around her. Stars still twinkled overhead, but the quarter moon was waning.

Maya located her car, then caught a sound much closer to the ground than the palm fronds.

She snapped her head to the right. For a woman who'd lived in Miami most of her life, it was an automatic response. Big-city girl, big-time guard.

For a moment there was nothing; then she caught a crunch of pebbles to her left. The black blur sprang at her before she could turn. It hit her hard and tackled her to the side of a large truck.

The impact knocked the air from her lungs. Her head slammed against the window; her shoulder against the metal frame.

Her assailant was bigger than her, Maya noted. Bigger, heavier and with momentum on his side.

But she'd lived with a cop; she knew how to evade the hand that tried to wrap around her throat.

Using her heel, she spiked his instep. Then she shoved her knee into his groin. She heard a rough hitch of breath and recognized the pain beneath it.

He slapped her back with his arm, and this time when her head hit, stars glittered.

She shook it off, had to. If she didn't, he'd catch her with the next blow. Keys, she thought and, twisting sideways, freed her right hand.

She heard a snarl as he attempted to pin her. She hadn't spied a weapon yet, but it would be a moot point if he got his fingers around her throat.

In the back of her mind, Maya registered a beam of light. It made him hesitate. It got him looking.

It gave her a chance.

He stopped her from stabbing his throat with her keys at the last second but forgot about the larger threat. While they wrestled, she rammed her knee full force between his legs.

He released her, with a curse, muffled by the black balaclava over his face.

Another light pierced the darkness. Swearing, he clutched his crotch. Then he dropped back, darted a look in both directions and bolted.

Ignoring the pain in her head and shoulder, Maya shoved away from the truck and ran in the opposite direction.

She grabbed her cell phone from her bag. Should she call 911 or Tal? After a quick debate, she went with the preferred option.

Did it even ring before he answered?

"Tal?"

"Stop running, Maya."

"What? How do you know…?" With the phone pressed to her ear, and still heading for the hospital, she swung in a circle. "Where are you?"

The collision brought her up short. If his reflexes

hadn't been a split second quicker than hers, she'd have kneed him dead center.

"Right behind you," Tal said from the depths of a long shadow. The hands that trapped her arms held her away from him just far enough to avoid injury. "You have really good aim, Dr. Santino."

She exhaled on a shaky curse. "You have even better timing, Lieutenant Talbot." Then she whirled. "Did you see him? The guy in the balaclava? He pushed me into the side of that truck."

Tal followed her gaze and shook his head. "All I saw was you running across the lot."

"Which I was doing because some thug dressed in black tried to have a football scrum with me." As her heart rate slowed, she picked out the booth near the entrance. "And, of course, Eddie's on a break."

"Eddie being the parking attendant?" Tal seemed more interested in scanning the lot than in finding the missing man.

Maya worked on uncoiling the tension knots in her throat, an easy feat in theory, not quite so simple in practice, with Tal's fingers still curled around her arms.

"I'm okay." She gave a gentle pull. "Nothing but a headache and a few bruises. My wannabe linebacker's probably in more pain right now than I am."

Tal's lips curved, though his eyes continued to probe the shadows. "Adam teach you how to kick?"

"Sorry to say it was my cousin Diego."

"The one with the speech impediment?"

"That's my cousin Jesus. Diego opens beer bottles by breaking their little glass necks and drinking from the splintered end. Shows how tough he is." She managed a smile. "You can stop searching. The guy's long gone.

He didn't get my purse or my medical bag. And don't look at me like that, because if you think he was trying to push me into the truck, I promise you, he wasn't."

"I know."

"I thought you might. Damn." She let her head fall back. "All things considered, this has been a really pissy night. You're going to tell me the attack was connected to Adam, aren't you?"

The gray eyes that returned to her face revealed nothing—which was so typically Tal, she didn't even bother to be irritated. "That's the part I wasn't going to tell you."

He smelled really good. Maya had no idea why she noticed that, but there it was, together with his very dark, very long hair; a two-day growth of stubble; and the kind of lean, hollowed-out features that made females from nineteen to ninety hot, flustered and more than a little tingly inside.

Thankfully, experience had taught her how to offset desire. That plus an overdose of fear.

She gave Tal's wrists a light tap. "Let go, Lieutenant. I'm not on the verge of collapse. Might sway a little after everything that's happened today, but we've all been there, right?"

"Are you babbling?"

"Not really." She resisted an urge to brush at his hair. "Babbling's an avoidance technique I never quite mastered. What I'm doing is stalling." Glancing away, she sighed, "What was Adam doing, Tal? What was he into that got him killed and me attacked? All I know is that it involves Orlando Perine."

"A man whose company just donated five hundred K to your hospital fund."

"Good PR for a straight corporate mogul, closer to blood money if McGraw's take on him is right," she noted.

"It is."

She blew out a long breath. "Anything else I should know?"

"One thing." Tal kept his eyes steady on hers. "Perine got married two weeks ago. Quietly and with only three people in attendance—the bride's mother, her brother and her stepfather, who just happens to be our deputy chief of police."

Chapter Three

He took her to a diner out on a disused two-lane highway that wound inland from the coast. Maya was so preoccupied, she barely noticed the beautiful sunrise, let alone the fifties-style Airstream structure.

Orlando Perine's stepfather-in-law was the deputy police chief. If the situation hadn't been so absurd, she would have laughed. She almost did, anyway, but that was either borderline hysteria or a brain so tired, it could no longer function. Since her eyes felt gritty and unfocused, she went with the latter.

A bell above the diner door jingled when Tal opened it. She smelled pancakes and, thank God, coffee as she preceded him inside.

"Okay, I'll accept that I'm not dreaming, though I was really hoping that would be the case here. Adam's gone, I'm in danger and Orlando Perine's not entirely straight. I know that sounds clinical, Tal, but this really doesn't want to sink in for me."

"Breathe deep enough, long enough, and it will," he replied.

"So you, what, infuse your resistant right hemisphere with so much oxygen that the vaguely surreal mutates into harsh reality? And we wonder why some people turn to drugs."

"Good thing you're not some people."

"Always the flatterer. But I wouldn't say no to a hit of caffeine."

As she spoke, Maya finally noticed the retro booths, the long counter with its row of red swivel stools and the scattering of pink flamingo napkin holders.

Tal steered her toward a table in the back.

The counterman came over, filled two coffee cups without asking and winked at Tal. "Better than your usual companion, Lieutenant. This one's a pinup." He took an appreciative sniff. "Smells like tropical spice."

After a hectic night in the E.R., Maya embraced the compliment. With her chin propped on her fist, she arched a brow at Tal. "Okay, what's the story, Lieutenant? You didn't bring me here so we could eat a healthy breakfast, and you've already dropped your bombshell. What's left that falls within the parameters of cop facts a civilian can be told?"

"Not a bad question for someone who's been up more than twenty-four hours."

"Adrenaline'll do that." She scanned the diner, her eyes straying to the counterman, who was holding court by the stools. "What did your friend over there mean by 'better than your usual companion'?"

A smile grazed Tal's lips. "Caught that, huh? He meant Nate Hammond. You've met him. Grizzled, crusty, cantankerous. Short on words, long on experience. He worked vice and fraud in his day. Captain in both departments. He was offered a promotion but decided he'd rather retire. Überstress versus a fishing pole. We do coffee stops and poker when we can."

A picture formed in Maya's head of a no-nonsense cop with a whiskey-and-cigarette voice and the occasional, if you looked really close, twinkle in his eyes.

"He used to come to blackjack nights when Adam and I lived in North Miami. Carried a battered red thermos of whiskey masquerading as iced tea."

"Only when he was off duty, and there was no masquerade. He just didn't want to spring for a flask."

Leaning forward on her arms, she said, "Talk to me, Tal. Tell me what's going on, what happened and why. If that guy in the parking lot attacked me because of Adam, I deserve an answer, and screw your cop rules."

Under scrutiny from Tal's gray eyes, she had to work to keep her features composed and her body language unrevealing. If she let her gaze stray to his mouth, even for a moment, she'd want to grab him and kiss him. After all these years, she'd have thought the urge would be gone, but surprisingly it wasn't. She wanted him as much now as she had back, well, back in another time.

"Sure you're up for this?" Tal asked.

"I have to be, don't I?" She drew circles on the table. "I don't want Adam to be dead, Tal. At my angriest, I never wanted that. I'm not sure…or, well, maybe I am. We shouldn't have gotten married. But we did. Things happened, and we split. I figure better our mistake than my parents'."

Something flickered in Tal's eyes. Understanding? Empathy? Desire?

He studied her, half-lidded. "Do you remember your father?"

This wasn't exactly how she'd envisioned their conversation going. But then, life was all about twists and turns and faded lines. "He left when I was three. In the summer, I think. I only have a vague memory of his face. My mother tossed all his pictures. Actually, she burned them, but that's the Latin temperament for you. Exorcise the mad any way you can." She selected a peach muffin from the basket the counterman had placed on their table, and spooned fresh marmalade on top. "I didn't really know him, so it wasn't as sad as it could have been."

"You've never heard from him?"

She shook her head. "Maybe he's dead. Maybe he isn't. I don't imagine I'll ever know."

Tal drank his coffee, continued to unsettle her with his cool gray stare. "Life tends to surprise, Maya. He could show up at that charity volleyball game you're playing on Sunday."

"Heard about that, huh?" Why wasn't she surprised? "Eden Bay vs. General. Jamie's our coach, but the smart money's on General. Do you know Jamie?"

"Tall woman, buzz-cut hair, has a wild kid going through a rebellious biker phase. I've seen them at the station."

"Renita's a handful."

"Unlike you at that age."

Maya laughed and felt better. "I was two handfuls, because I happened to be crazy about the high school bad boy."

"You liked the bad boy, and yet you married Adam. Not sure what that says about you, Maya."

"I think it says I've changed. Kids grow up. In fact, my bad boy's a loan officer now. Drives a Volvo. And Adam…" Her eyes locked on his. "Tal, why is Adam dead?"

She knew he was weighing his answer. "Adam made a deal, with one of Perine's men," he finally said.

"What kind of deal?"

"For information, facts and figures, incriminating evidence."

"Pertaining to?"

"Real estate fraud, investment fraud, development fraud, counterfeiting."

"Okay, I get the fraud part, that's why Adam was after him. But you must have known or at least suspected he might also be a murderer."

"Homicide and fraud were cooperating on the investigation."

"Big fish, small pond," Maya recalled. At Tal's arched brow, she opened her mind to the full horrible memory. "Adam said that just before he died. I forgot about it, or maybe I buried it."

"Reverse the adjectives and you've got McGraw." Tal stroked her inner wrist. "I know this is hard for you, Maya, but you'll have to go through it when you give your statement anyway."

"I know. He said I shouldn't trust anyone, anywhere." A smile stole across her lips. "Considering the deputy chief connection, he was probably right. He didn't say much else, really, just told me to tell you to seal the deal. Guess that means you're the only person I can trust, huh?"

"Guess so."

She wanted him to touch her again. When he didn't, she asked, "What was McGraw's status relative to Adam's?"

"Adam was in charge."

"And now?"

"It's a homicide. Pushes McGraw even farther down the authority ladder."

"I can't see that sitting well. Who's heading the investigation now?"

"Drake's still pulling files, juggling."

"Do you have any idea who Perine's triggerman is?"

He glanced at the surrounding tables, all occupied by diners.

"It can wait," Maya said when Tal brought his gaze back. "Going back to the father thing, I know you have some issues there yourself." Her eyes danced. "I love that word, don't you? No one has problems anymore. It's all about issues." She fingered her long pendant. "It's about memories, too, isn't it? Not the best for either of us, it seems."

"Makes us simpatico," he said, with an odd tone in his voice. Sarcasm? Bitterness? Regret? "Could be that's what triggered Adam's jealousy."

"Oh, good. Guilt." Maya smiled. "Rewind to Orlando Perine." Cognizant of the people beside them, she lowered her voice. "I talked to the M.E. last night, during a lull. He extracted two bullets from Adam's body. Will those bullets tell you anything about the killer?"

Tal ran a finger along her arm, from her wrist to her elbow, and drew a shiver. "They already have."

Okay. She should withdraw. Now. Ignore the shiver in her belly and send him a message. Instead, she arched a brow. "You're doing this on purpose, aren't you?"

"Could be."

"Why?"

"Because I don't like being the bearer of bad news."

"And that is?"

"The gun used to murder Adam was also used to murder two other people. One of them was an investment broker named Gund."

Despite the chill that feathered down her spine, Maya managed a calm, "And the other?"

"Was the person who found him. Apparently, Gund wasn't quite dead when the finder got there."

"I'm not going to like this, am I?"

"It's why I came back to the hospital, Maya." Now he trapped her fingers in his hands. "Fraud wasn't as cooperative about the Perine investigation as we were led to believe. We weren't given the connection."

"Nice of them to finally share. Ah, about this person who found Gund not quite dead—?"

"Her name was Ellen Latimer. She'd been driving taxis for twenty years. No work-related assaults, only a handful of minor accidents, no injuries. According to the file Captain Drake managed to access last night, she was killed in her taxi less than three hours after Gund was pronounced dead. Someone shot her in the back of the head."

A FULL TWELVE HOURS AFTER driving Maya to her South Miami home, Tal continued to curse himself.

He should have waited in the hospital lounge, but the autopsy report had been rushed through and the results e-mailed to his captain. Drake had insisted he return to the station to examine the report and go over the file he'd strong-armed away from fraud. One look inside, and Tal had floored it back to Eden Bay.

He'd tried to call Maya en route, but with the E.R. in an uproar, getting through had been impossible.

He'd missed her by five minutes. Five. And in those minutes, one of Perine's men, possibly the one who'd killed Adam, had jumped her. Good thing for her, she knew how to knee a man.

Now Tal was in his captain's office, filling him in on the file.

"Did McGraw know about the taxi driver?" he asked.

"Don't know how much anyone other than Adam was really in the loop."

Though he was rereading the report, Tal's mind remained on Maya. "You've got guys on her, right?"

Drake jabbed his computer keyboard. "She's safe. I didn't send rookies to guard her. I'm sorry, but I can't spare you for protection detail. Besides, you're the one who told me she wouldn't want a cop camping out in her living room."

She wouldn't want to stop living her life, either, and that, Tal reflected, was where the real problem resided.

"She a good doctor?" Drake asked.

Tal half smiled. "Top of her class."

"Florida State?"

"With a premed at Yale."

"Impressive." Drake leaned back in his chair. "Is she as pretty as I've heard?"

"Depends what you've heard."

"The word *stunning* has come up. Knockout. Killer body." At Tal's slanted look, he let out a heavy breath. "I know, we've got an unholy mess on our hands with the deputy chief, with Tyler, with Perine."

"We've also got two victims we didn't know about until last night."

"Those homicides occurred outside our jurisdiction. Outside fraud's as well, but we'll assume they had some kind of deal going there."

Tal drained the coffee he'd poured earlier. For the moment, he had no choice. He had to trust the men Drake had put on Maya. She lived in a secure condominium complex. Good alarm, decent neighbors, solid cops. She'd be safe. He hoped.

His cell phone beeped as he was going through the

report for a third time. He regarded the screen, smiled faintly at the name.

"Hey, Nate. What's up?"

The older cop's voice sounded more gravelly than usual. "Heard you boys have a problem."

"You could say that."

"You back in Miami for good?"

"Until the investigation's done."

In the background, Drake made a rough sound. "Tell Hammond to haul his ass down to central and see what he can shake loose from his old comrades. My gut says they're still withholding."

"Heard that," Nate remarked. "My advice would be to lean on McGraw. Let him think he's got a shot at moving up to homicide."

"Way ahead of you there." Tal started for the door. "McGraw's on his way over. Means I'm out of here. Anything useful for us in terms of Perine?"

"For the moment, only a keen ear and a full thermos. Come on over when you get a chance. We'll compare notes. Off the record, of course."

Another beep on Tal's cell phone indicated a second incoming call. This one from Maya.

"Hang on, Nate." He switched lines. "Thought you'd be sleeping, Doc."

"I was. It came to me at the end of a dream."

"What did?"

"The guy's face."

Tal angled away from the surrounding noise. "The one who jumped you?"

"No. He was wearing a balaclava. The man I'm talking about was with Adam. I think. He disappeared so fast, I almost didn't notice him. Look, can you come over? I'd come to you, except I seem to have left my car in the hospital parking lot."

The wall clock read 6:30 p.m. "Give me twenty minutes," he said. "I'll use the siren."

"Boys with toys. I'll do a sketch while I wait. Uh, Tal, should I feed the dynamic duo in the bushes outside?"

"They're fine. Keep your doors locked, Maya."

"Yes, Mommy."

He switched back to Nate as he shouldered the fire door open. "Gotta go, Nate. We'll unload that thermos another time when I'm off duty."

"You're too pure, Lieutenant."

"Only when it counts."

"Hang on, Tal. I didn't call to find myself a drinking partner. I was around that department for a lot of years. I saw stuff that'd make Drake's fringe of hair knot up. Perine's got people inside. That's how he does it. Forget the deputy chief connection for now. I'm talking long-term, longtime snitches, on Perine's payroll as well as the city's."

The suggestion didn't surprise Tal so much as the whip of contempt in Nate's voice.

"I take it you never found any specific evidence."

"Got within an inch some days, but no, I never could pin the greaseball turncoats down. Like Perine, they always managed to ooze through the cracks at the last second. Look for those cracks, Tal. Get to them before the ooze does. Do that, and you'll have your blue line to Perine. Won't be a straight one, but crooked's no problem for you."

Tal shoved through the outer door and put on his sunglasses to cut the low glare. He tossed his jacket inside his truck. "How many do you figure and what divisions?"

"No idea. Fraud for sure, probably homicide. Vice? Hard to say. Internal affairs? Unlikely, but you never know. I'd count on a handful of uniforms, maybe more."

Tal revved the engine, switched on the flashing lights. "I'm using the siren, Nate. It's gonna get loud. Have you talked to Drake about this?"

"Talked to Tyler a couple times, and his captain once, but Drake, no."

"Why?"

Nate made a rusty sound. "Don't get me wrong. I like the guy. We squared off a time or two as captains, but that's how it is. I trusted him when it mattered, and he came through."

With a look in both directions and the siren blaring, Tal maneuvered through an intersection. "You might want to get to the point here."

"Captains make decent money, but yours has five kids, and one of 'em's autistic."

"Nate…"

"Sneak a peek in his garage, Tal. Drive out to his place and take a good long look at Don Drake's brand-new, fully loaded flatbed truck."

Chapter Four

The sky over the ocean was on fire. Maya wanted to soak up the last of the summer rays, but there was little chance of that, with Jamie badgering her at full volume.

After five nonstop minutes, she simply reached out and set a hand across her friend's mouth. "Enough, okay? I appreciate the gesture, Jamie, but Tal's on his way over. That'll make three cops in the immediate area."

Jamie yanked Maya's hand away. "We're sitting on your balcony, facing a courtyard so much like the one in that movie about the photographer with the broken leg that it gives me the heebie-jeebies. How can you be flip?"

"I'm not being flip. And it was *Rear Window*."

"Do I care about titles?" Jamie spread her fingers. "I see a flock of weirdos down there and a window directly across from yours, with the shades drawn."

"That's Mr. Ruiz's place. He's—"

"Busy hacking up his wife's body? Phoning his female coconspirator? Polishing up his escape plan?"

Maya shot her an exasperated look. "Have you been stealing medication from the hospital? Mr. Ruiz is a night watchman at a large office complex. He sleeps during the day. See that big orange ball over there?" She pointed with her pencil. "That's the sun. Work all night, sleep all day."

"Maya, you were attacked early this morning in a public parking lot."

"I know. I was there. Do you want a glass of lemonade?"

"I'd rather have rum."

"Are you driving?"

"Knock-knock. I brought your car back. I'll cab it home."

Maya sat back. If there was a mental picture she didn't need to draw right then, it involved taxis and their drivers. In this case, a female driver, murdered because she'd stopped to help a not-quite-dead man who'd pissed off his boss in a big and apparently fatal way.

Setting her sketchbook aside, she went to stand at the balcony rail.

"There were no palm trees in *Rear Window*," she said over her shoulder. "It was also set in New York."

Jamie huffed out a breath. "I get your point. This isn't a movie. It's real life. I still think you could give me a hint about what's going on."

"Are you kidding? A hint's all *I've* been given so far."

"Sex him."

A laugh bubbled up. "Excuse me?"

"Use your body, Maya, your wiles, your brain if you have to, but get answers."

"All very complimentary in its own warped way, but I'm a doctor, and Tal's a cop. We're not john and undercover hooker here."

"So you're not curious?"

"I didn't say that."

"No, but... Oh, crap, I give up. You'll tell me what

you want to when you want to. Just please tell me you're still good to go for the game tomorrow. You're the best setter I've got."

Turning, Maya bumped a hip against the iron railing. "I'll be there, Coach Hazell. Might be bringing a few official friends, but I won't let you down."

"I'll settle for that." Jamie craned her neck sideways. "Whose face are you drawing? It looks like your hot lieutenant's."

"You have a good memory to go with your nursing skills." Maya lifted her own face to the setting sun. "Tal will be here any minute."

"My cue to exit stage right. Look, don't limit yourself, okay? You've got the bod. Use it. Knowledge is power. You can't trust other people to keep you safe. The best protection comes from within. Not that there are any real guarantees…about anything or anyone."

Maya heard the zip of Jamie's shoulder bag, saw something glint in her peripheral vision. When she looked back, her friend was smiling. Over the top of the gun she'd just removed from her bag.

TAL'S POLICE RADIO GAVE a static-filled squawk. He reached down to engage.

"Busy here, Carlisle."

"Aware of that, Talbot." The female dispatcher matched his irritable tone. "Captain thought you'd like to know that a patrol found Tyler's Mustang outside a waterfront warehouse. The Ricolini Brothers warehouse, to be exact. It's on its way to be impounded."

"Tell the tow guys that if they scratch it, they'll want to avoid me for a few months."

"It's only a car, for Chrissake."

"A classic car. Anything in the warehouse?"

"Yeah. Blood."

"Adam's?"

"That's the consensus. We'll know soon enough. I've got you en route to Dr. Maya Santino's. Captain wants you to escort her to the station ASAP."

"When I can."

He switched off, worked his way through a clogged intersection.

He kept seeing Maya's face, couldn't get it out of his head. Should he feel guilty about that? Probably not. Should he worry about it? Absolutely.

Because any objection he raised was merely a front for the real reason he'd kept his distance all these years.

In the few hours of sleep he'd managed to catch earlier today, that reason had come back in an all-too-familiar rush of twisted images and distorted memories. Of his mother and his father, of shouting matches and tears, of objects being hurled, of doors being slammed.

Near the end, the doors gave a metallic clang, and the shouts gave way to a squeal of tires on rain-soaked pavement.

It was the same nightmare, always the same. Windshield wipers slapping louder and louder. His mother's voice rising from a whisper to a cry as she reminded him that he'd only gotten half his genes from her. As she dragged him into the light and showed him the bruises…

Swearing, Tal shoved it away, concentrated on not killing anyone while he made a sharp left. Yes, Adam had been his friend, and, yes, there'd been problems between them. But guilt and friendship were merely excuses.

It was the bruises that mattered.

JAMIE HELD TIGHT TO THE gun, and to her conviction.

"Take it, Maya. It's old, not much, hardly more than a prop, actually, but no creep who jumps you in the dark will know that."

"Jamie, I've only been jumped by one creep in twenty-nine years." Unless you counted her cousin Diego, who'd leapfrogged over her during a treasure hunt at his ninth birthday party. "I have cops watching me, I know self-defense and I don't freak easily."

"A little extra protection can't hurt.'

"No guns, Jamie."

Her friend blew out a breath. "Your daddy must have been a mule."

Maya took the gun, unzipped Jamie's bag and dropped it inside. "I'm fine with firearms in their place. That place just isn't with me."

"Some kind of stinging spray then. Will you at least carry that?"

"Mommies everywhere," Maya murmured.

"What can I say?" Jamie hoisted her bag. "We worry."

Maya walked her through the living room. "Speaking of worry, how's your daughter?"

"She wants to be called Mask. Tell you anything?"

Maya told herself not to laugh. "Is there a reason?"

"Not that I've heard. Her therapist thinks I should enroll her in a twenty-four-week program. Great idea, until you look at the price tag. I reminded him that I'm a nurse, not a pro athlete."

"Listen, Jamie. I don't have kids, but I do have a little extra money. I could—"

Jamie cut her off sharply. "I don't borrow from friends. It fuddles things up." At a knock on the door,

Maya sighed, checked the viewer, then opened to Tal. Before she could speak, her friend gave a long whistle.

"Wow. You really are a hottie, aren't you, Lieutenant? Tall, dark and totally bootylicious."

Maya hooked her fingers in Jamie's waistband. "Roll up your tongue, Nurse Hazell, and say goodbye to the nice lieutenant."

Jamie grimaced. "You really know how to butcher a moment, don't you? Keep her safe, Lieutenant Talbot. Good E.R. doctors are hard to come by."

Tal stood aside so she could make her exit, but remained on the threshold, with his shoulder resting on the door frame. "You look refreshed, Dr. Santino."

"You don't. Showered and changed, yes. Like a man who got more than three hours of sleep, no."

"Two, but I'll make up for it." He stepped inside, looked around. "Tell me about your dream."

She leaned against the closed door. "It wasn't a dream so much as a flash of memory. I went outside to see how many patients still needed attention and saw them. Someone was shaking Adam. He stopped when he saw me and took off. There were a lot of shadows, Tal, and I was more concerned about Adam than the person with him."

"But you saw his face."

"Enough to sketch it. My mother was a painter. I didn't inherit her talent, but I can draw passable features." Including his, she reflected, far more often than she should. "My sketchbook's on the balcony."

She knew he was watching her. She felt his eyes on her back, on her bare arms and legs, on the ponytail, which she wore to combat the heat.

Without turning, she called back, "Stop looking at

my butt, Tal. You're—" she opted for one of Jamie's words and a slow smile "—fuddling me."

"No comment," he murmured and unsnapped his shoulder holster.

When she faced him again, she took in his long dark hair; his jeans, which hugged in all the right places; and boots that had seen better days.

So who was looking now?

Retrieving her sketchbook, Maya flipped to the last page. Tal was so close on her heels, she would have crashed into him if she'd taken a single step back.

"Guess we're staying out here." She slapped the sketchbook against his chest before he could take the step she hadn't. "I'm not ready for you, Tal. Not even close to ready."

He held her in place with his eyes. It was a gift he'd always possessed and, in its own way, a powerful weapon where females were concerned, though she'd seen him stare down more than a few men.

In spite of herself, she couldn't stop a laugh from climbing into her throat. "God, but you're making this hard."

"Why the defensive posture, Doc?" The ghost of a smile appeared on his face as he ran a light hand along her arm. "I haven't done anything yet."

She kept her hand on his chest. "I never wished anything bad for Adam."

"I never thought you did. Neither did he."

"I loved him. I think. In a college-student-meets-cop sort of way." Something uncoiled inside her with the admission. "Well, that's weird. I tell you something I should feel bad about, and I feel better instead."

"We're complex creatures, Maya."

"You and me in particular, or humans in general?"

"Six of one."

Her heart beat harder, louder, faster the longer he stared. She couldn't drag her eyes from his mouth. More than anything right then, she wanted that mouth on hers. Out of nowhere it occurred to her that she was arching backward, over the rail, a dangerous position in more ways than one. Still, what was life without a little danger?

He wrapped his fingers around her nape. "Don't worry, Doc. I won't let you fall."

Then he covered her mouth with his, and sent every emotion inside her over the edge.

THE SKETCHBOOK LANDED on the floor of the balcony, between them. Tal heard the thud as he held her face between his fingers and deepened the kiss.

He shouldn't have done it. Signals flashed in his head. *Back off. Fast. Do it.* The warnings were similar to the ones Adam had issued to every man who'd seen her. To every man, like Tal, who'd wanted her.

He tasted her now with his tongue, thought of a rare and potent wine. The first sip drew him in. It deepened the hunger, which had been there since they'd met, fueled his desire and seduced him in a way even strong friendship couldn't offset.

It surprised him a little that she kissed him back. He'd expected her to push him away, to put him off and tell him it couldn't happen. Instead, her fingers tangled in his hair and held.

He angled his head in response, explored her mouth more thoroughly. Oh, yeah, definitely wine. Wild, forbidden, too tempting to resist. And Tal could resist a lot.

Only Maya had ever gotten past his formidable guard. Only Maya had the power to scare the living hell out of him.

Reason enough to stop kissing her, to back off and call it a mistake.

She slid her hands to his waist and drew his lower lip into her mouth before she rested her forehead against his.

The taste of her lingered. It took a huge effort to wrap his fingers around her upper arms, shield his expression and look into her eyes.

"You feel like you're trespassing, don't you?"

Her question surprised him. "Do I?"

"I think so. And you would have been once. But not now. Not for a very long time."

"So why did you stop?"

She ran her finger over his lower lip, replaced it with her mouth. When she licked him, his brain, already overheated, turned to mush. "Pausing isn't stopping."

"Maya..."

The argument died. Later, when he was alone and half-sane, he'd be all over it, but for now, he simply wanted to cage his conscience and let the fantasy ride.

She kissed him this time, used her teeth, her lips, her tongue.

Greed set in, chased by hunger. He'd been hard before he touched her, and now she was touching him, running her hands over his jeans, frying every thought in his brain.

Blood pounded through him like a drum. He dragged her closer, heard her purr, felt her hips rub against him.

He'd have breathed if he could, but something other than air had gotten into his lungs. Something that punched through the snapping threads of his control.

Tal had no idea where things might have gone from there. However, drugged or not, he recognized the blast below them in an instant.

Maya tore her mouth free, whipped her eyes down. "Was that…?"

"Yeah, it was." Shoving her behind him, Tal grabbed the backup from his waistband.

And searched the courtyard for the person who'd fired the gun.

"IT WAS AN ACCIDENT, I swear. I took the safety off, like so. But there was a pain in my wrist. Then, oh no, the gun, it dropped, and kaboom. It went off."

Maya's neighbor, the man with the drawn shades, appealed primarily to her, although his nervous eyes kept flitting to Tal.

"Please, Dr. Santino." Carl Ruiz adopted an attitude of prayer. "Tell the officer I didn't mean to do it."

"It's all right, Carl." Maya attempted to calm him. "Lieutenant Talbot knows you work as a security guard."

"For six months," the man put in. "I hit my hand on the counter yesterday and hurt the bone. I'm sorry to have caused so much trouble…."

Thirty minutes and several reassurances later, Maya and Tal left the man's apartment and made their way back to the courtyard.

The people who'd reacted to the gunshot had returned to their tasks and chores, leaving the area empty.

Maya turned a curious half circle as she walked. "Where are my bodyguards? Please say they're not skulking around Mr. Ruiz's place, because I promise you, that man is not on Orlando Perine's payroll."

"Anyone could be on Perine's payroll, Maya."

"Tal, he's sixty-eight years old."

"Nate arrested a man in his seventies three years ago who was part of a money-laundering op."

"Perine's op?"

"Odds are. Don't trust anyone, anywhere, remember."

"This is why I didn't become a cop. I'd have failed Cynicism 101 miserably." She nudged him and almost drew a smile. "Look, it's eight o'clock. Why don't we go somewhere for dinner, and you can tell me all the dirty details surrounding Adam's death. In return, I'll show you my sketch of the man I think might have brought him to the hospital. Because we know he didn't drive himself, and I'm betting no taxi company in the city has a record of doing it, either."

Tal's eyes narrowed. "And you know we checked because?"

"You're too thorough to overlook something so obvious." She climbed the outside stairs, ahead of him. "When you live with a cop for three years, stuff rubs off."

"Make it through Cynicism 101, Dr. S., and you're in."

"Rather keep my day job. Since you didn't answer about dinner, I'll go out on a limb and speculate that your captain has a somewhat different evening planned for me. Like, say, staring at a million photos, answering a ton of questions and giving a weighty statement?"

"Did I mention that Internal Affairs is in the market for a couple of detectives?"

"That's a no to the food, then." She tugged the black scrunchie from her hair. "I hope your captain likes pizza."

STAY CALM, STAY CENTERED, stay hidden.

The words became Falcon's mantra. Except when

panic took over, and he found himself jumping at the sound of a flushed toilet upstairs. Then he knew he had to change locations, before he wound up flushed out to sea.

The information was still in limbo—it had to be—floating between wherever Tyler had stashed it and his own desperate fingers. Get it back, and he'd be set. Lose it to the higher power, and he might as well put a bullet in his head right now.

His life hinged on that information. And the woman. The dead doctor who, by some miracle, continued to walk around.

When a second toilet flushed, Falcon's pulse spiked. Letting out a laugh, he banged his head against the wall. He'd turned his back on Orlando Perine for this? What the hell had he been thinking? Forget the doctor. He was the walking dead himself. Or very soon would be.

He banged his head again to make himself focus.

The information *was* out there. If not, the big man would have been arrested. No connection in the world would stop that from happening. So there really was a chance. As long as the big man walked free, the dead could skulk along in his shadow.

Falcon pressed his sweaty forehead to the wall. He didn't have to die. He simply had to return the information. He had to get to Tyler's ex. Before the beautiful doctor wound up shot and flushed.

One lovely body part at a time.

Chapter Five

"That was an adventure," Maya remarked three hours later, as they drove through a still-lively Little Havana. "The only thing missing from Captain Drake's party was a lineup."

"Lineups require suspects," Tal reminded her.

"So, still a possibility."

"Most unpleasant things are where Drake's concerned."

"I suppose you can't fault thoroughness."

Tal indicated a busy outdoor restaurant. "Still hungry?"

Although Maya's body wanted to rock to the beat of a nearby marimba band, her mind felt more fried than juiced. "Ravenous, but I have frijoles and sangria at my place. We can eat on the balcony, and you can tell me all about Falcon."

"Caught the name, huh?"

"More than once, which says to me that he is or was Adam's informant and very likely the man who brought him to the hospital. Sorry to say, your Falcon looks more like a half-starved rat than a bird of prey."

"He probably chose the code name."

"Any idea how he fits into Perine's organization?"

"No, but we'll circulate your description and his picture."

She glanced over, smiled. "Will you be circulating that picture through the deputy police chief's office?"

Tal's lips twitched. "Hanley's taking copies of the sketch over there tomorrow."

"And Hanley is?"

"Dolores Hanley. You met her when Adam and I were sergeants and she was a lieutenant in Vice. She made captain when Nate retired."

A face popped into Maya's head, of a middle-aged woman with black hair, piercing eyes and long, strong limbs. "I remember. We met at a Christmas party. She told me to call her Dolly and, God, I think we did a foxtrot together, because we'd been drinking and none of the men there danced." Setting that memory aside, Maya allowed another one in. "Tal, do all the cops in the department know about Adam?"

"All the cops in the country know. Or will the minute they're back in the communication loop."

"One of your own." She watched a woman in a skintight dress gesture rudely at her companion on a narrow strip of sidewalk. "Adam said the deal was yours to finish, but he didn't mention any information. All he said was that I shouldn't trust anyone, and then that thing about big fish in small ponds."

"And so we wind our way back to clichés."

"Well, yeah." She slanted him a meaningful look. "Or clues."

"If you're casting our deputy chief in the role of the big fish, my guess is it's too blatant."

"Ah, so clues have to be subtle?"

He cast her a wry glance. "Adam was probably trying

to tell you as little as possible in order to minimize the danger to your life. Hero types do that kind of thing."

"A laudable attitude, except whoever attacked me in the hospital parking lot has no idea what Adam did or didn't say. So for all the difference it makes, he might as well have been blatant." She frowned, twisted in her seat. "Uh, Tal, that man over there is holding a knife."

Tal flicked a look at a tall, skinny man in a backward cap who was making quick air jabs at his male companion with a jackknife.

"The Buchanan cousins. They do this all the time."

"Threaten each other at knifepoint?"

"Screwdriver point. They bet on rival baseball teams. A few tequilas postgame and out come the drivers."

Maya made an oblique hand motion. "And that's, like, cool with you men in blue?"

"We're a thin blue line, Doc. You know what it is to be short staffed. Next patrol that passes will probably have a few things to say."

She let it go. Tal knew the Miami streets. He also knew people, individuals and types. In many ways, she thought, he'd have made a good doctor.

Bonnie Raitt played softly on the car radio. Outside, the night heat carried a hint of ocean breeze. Not enough to cool it, but the scent was there, mixed with the smell of warm pavement, palm trees and buildings baked by the summer sun.

Maya's gaze lowered from the moon overhead to Tal's face in profile.

She needed help; she really did. Even tired and hungry, she still wanted to kiss him. The human mind might fascinate, but not as much as Stephen Talbot.

Several silent seconds passed before she ventured a soft "Are you going to drive it?"

"The Mustang? Yeah. We rebuilt the engine together, Maya, restored the body. Modified and customized the interior. You don't do that to a vehicle, then let it sit."

"My great-uncle Pedro lets his motorcycle sit."

"Isn't your great-uncle Pedro eighty-five years old?"

"So?"

"With a record of street racing, for which he was ticketed six months ago?"

"Adam had no life if Uncle Pedro's driving record was the best he could come up with for beer-at-the-bar conversation."

"He had his license yanked, didn't he?"

Maya refused to laugh. "You're completely missing the point, Lieutenant."

He grinned. "No, I get it. I just think you're pretty when you're riled."

"I don't get riled over eccentric relatives. Now, if you want to talk about Cousin Diego…"

"Why don't we talk about Adam's condo instead? Do you plan to sell it or keep it?"

"Assuming Adam's brother and sister don't challenge the will, I'll probably sell it." She started to lift her hair off her neck but stopped the motion partway. "Now, there's an interesting conga line."

Tal watched a group of young people jostle each other in a crosswalk. "Not much of a conga line."

Maya unfastened her seat belt, leaned over and turned Tal's head to the left. "Snap, Lieutenant. Unless I'm hallucinating, Orlando Perine and his human armada are currently parading through the side door of the Marbel Club." Her amusement swelled. "And just look who's on their collective heels. One hard-boiled fraud detective, sporting a gleam that could light up the harbor."

With a similar gleam, Tal switched on his flashing lights and made a quick U-turn. "I hope you're in the mood to dance."

"I DON'T NEED YOUR PERMISSION to be here." McGraw started to poke a finger at Tal's chest but changed his mind when he spotted the glimmer in Tal's eyes. "Did you follow me here?" he demanded.

Tal continued to stare, leaving Maya to answer. "If we had, it would have been a more enjoyable experience than the one we had downtown, poring over mug shots, answering questions and ingesting stale coffee."

McGraw's lip curled. "Always an editorial, Ms. Santori."

"*Doctor* Santino," Tal corrected softly. "A title earned, Quick Draw...."

McGraw's lips tightened. "Tyler was your friend and my colleague. Like it or not—and trust me, at this moment I don't—we're kith and kin within the department." He glared at Maya. "Tyler was also your husband. You'll have to excuse me, but I intend to do whatever I have to in order to nail his killer."

Maya's smile was benign. "To get his killer, Detective, or to cash in on his death? From my vantage point, it looks like you're trying to prove to someone—Captain Drake, I presume—what a crack investigator you are. Worthy of promotion or transfer... By the way, if either of you is interested, Perine and his bodyguards have settled into a booth at the back of the room."

McGraw would have made a beeline for the open staircase if Tal hadn't nabbed his arm.

"Before you blast off, Gene, give me an idea of what questions you plan to ask."

"Let me think. Oh, yes, I thought I'd start with the usual where, when and with who at the time of the murder. You know, what we in the trade call procedure."

"We know where he was, McGraw."

"We know where he says he was. Aboard his yacht, with his collection of well-paid cretins. FYI, his new wife flew to Tallahassee three days ago with her sister."

Tal tossed a glance at the floor below. "You think he still pulls his own triggers?"

"He has," said McGraw.

"Yeah, back when Crockett and Tubbs were cruising the streets of Miami. The world's changed since then and so has Perine's MO."

While the two men engaged in yet another testosterone-based argument, Maya let the music divert her. The edgy mix of Queen meets South American hip-hop had a compelling beat.

While part of her wanted to lure Tal onto the dance floor, she knew McGraw would jump all over that.

On the other hand, how could a single sexy dance hurt anything? They could sway to the music, the beginnings of a suggestive samba now, and keep an eye on Orlando Perine at the same time.

Homing back in on her surroundings, she realized she'd drifted in body as well as thought along the walkway. Probably just as well, since Tal and McGraw had gone from throwing invisible daggers to shooting invisible bullets.

Should she break it up or wait until the real bullets appeared? Maya was debating the pros and cons when a pair of hands snaked out of the darkness behind her.

"Not a word, Dr. Santino," a man's voice warned in her ear.

With his fingers clamped to her arms, he pulled her from the railing and shoved her toward the black end of the walkway.

"SCUM LIKE PERINE AREN'T big on MOs, Lieutenant. Opportunity and results, that's what it's all about. And not getting caught."

Which was an MO in its own right, but Tal didn't bother to point it out. He was more curious to know what McGraw had planned to accomplish by dogging Perine to the Marbel Club.

The detective aimed a look of disgust at the floor below. "The guy's fingering us, Talbot. He knows we know he owns a good third of the bars and restaurants in Little Havana, and he's jerking us sideways by making the rounds. Like any conscientious business owner would."

"You think that, then you haven't met many business owners. Most of them don't even live in the country."

"Proves my point, doesn't it? Perine's bending over backward to convince us he's straight, when we know he's dirty."

Tal's gaze slid to the railing where Maya was observing the action below. He frowned. Where she'd *been* observing the action. The only people there now were an Asian couple and a six-pack of bearded bikers.

Tal's brain snapped to attention. Had she gone to the washroom? Spotted a friend? Ditched the squabbling cops and taken a taxi home?

His instincts said no to all of it. She wouldn't leave without telling him. Not on her own at any rate.

Swearing, he shoved past McGraw's arm.

The detective's disgruntled sneer turned to an uncomprehending scowl. "Why the rush? Is someone dead?"

"He better hope not." Tal probed the shadows, spotted her, nodded forward even as he reached under his jacket for his gun. "That guy's got Maya."

McGraw followed his gaze. "One of Perine's goons?"

"Looks like. Take the south staircase." Tal started off at a run. "Intercept him before he reaches the exit."

Or wherever the hell Perine's oversized ghoul was taking her.

His eyes adjusted quickly to the darkness on the walkway. The man was pushing Maya ahead of him. He had her left arm trapped and his right hand pressed to her spine. He had a gun, Tal judged, or a knife. Some kind of weapon, anyway. Maya was making it difficult for him, but she wasn't struggling as hard as he suspected she could.

Perine's table sat across the dance floor, away from the stairs. Using the shadows together with the people on the treads, Tal closed in.

Sizing up the distance, he went for it and vaulted over the railing, to the floor. He caught up easily as Perine's man endeavored to maneuver his captive around the top of the dance floor.

The music was sultry now. Lasers flashed from light to dark and back, as if ribbons of color were being woven between them.

The man dragged Maya along the upper rim of the room, as far away from the dance floor as possible.

Tal's adrenaline surged. Three, two, one. Raising his arm, he stepped out of the shadow and pressed his gun into the henchman's neck.

In a single smooth motion, he reached around and freed Maya. "Good freeze," he congratulated. "Now let's keep walking and see where the three of us wind up."

"I'M SORRY FOR THE misunderstanding, Dr. Santino, Lieutenant Talbot." On his feet, Orlando Perine extended a square, slightly calloused hand. "Please, have a seat while we sort out this unfortunate misunderstanding."

"Well, hello there, Mr. Perine," a new voice boomed. "Up to your usual tricks, are you?"

Maya managed, barely, to keep a straight face when Gene McGraw strode into view. He made a show of tucking his gun away, and no attempt to keep his voice down.

"Doing a little kidnapping on the side these days, are we, O.P.?"

Perine's expression didn't falter. Neither did his smooth tone. "You must be Detective Sergeant McGraw."

"So, you know me, then?"

"Of you, certainly. As I recall, you tried to bully your way into my wedding reception. Then there was the attempted invasion of a board meeting at my waterfront restaurant three weeks ago, and the minor furor you created at my casino last weekend."

Before McGraw could respond, Perine turned his attention to Tal. "I can feel your eyes boring into me, Lieutenant. That's quite a gift you possess. My father... Ah, but I don't suppose you're interested in a story of a Mexican farmer who settled in Manatee County and grew oranges for a living. Six children, no wife. Died far too young."

"Why?" was all Tal said, and for the first time since they'd arrived, Perine shot his bodyguard a grim look.

"As I said earlier, it was a misunderstanding. Or perhaps I should say a miscommunication. I saw Dr. Santino on the walkway and wanted to have a word with her. I'm sure you're aware that we're on the board of Eden Bay Hospital."

"So you sent Lurch here to strong-arm her down."

"My man mistook the request. It happens, Lieutenant Talbot."

McGraw revved up. Before he could go off, Maya asked, "What did you want to see me about, Mr. Perine?"

Perine's gaze ran the circle. "Perhaps now isn't the best time to go into it."

Tal's smile was a match for Maya's. "So we'll just arrest your man here and call it a night, shall we?"

Perine spread his fingers. "I see no reason to be difficult, Lieutenant. My man will be dealt with."

"Good to know," replied Tal. "Tell me, Mr. Perine, are you acquainted with the Ricolini Brothers?"

"I've used their shipping and storage services a number of times."

McGraw glowered. "What the lieutenant means is—"

"I know what he means, Detective Sergeant. I read the newspaper as well as the next person. I'm sorry about your friend." Perine turned to Maya. "Believe it or not, I respected Adam Tyler."

Tal studied his face. Maya knew he was looking for the unconscious muscle twitches that often gave people away. Perine would have most of them covered, but you never knew what might slip through.

"Adam was a good cop," Tal agreed in a mild tone. "Almost as good as Nate Hammond in his day."

"Oh, but there aren't many as good as Captain

Hammond, are there, Lieutenant? Or Drake. Cream rises in all fields of endeavor." Perine refocused on Maya. "I assume your ex-husband left his possessions to you."

"Some of them."

"And you were the last person to see him, to speak to him?"

"I was, yes."

"It must have been difficult for you."

"Death is always difficult, Mr. Perine. The death of an ex-spouse unleashes a unique kind of sadness."

"Were you close as ex-spouses?"

"No." She smiled. "But I was still the last person Adam spoke to."

At a subtle look from his boss, the man who'd grabbed her on the walkway cleared his throat. "I'm, uh, sorry if I hurt you, Dr. Santino. I didn't mean to be so rough."

"The implication being that you'll be gentler the next time?" McGraw cocked a brow. "Good to be fore-warned, isn't it, Doc?"

"As much as possible," she agreed. "Any hospital-related matter can be dealt with on Monday, Mr. Perine." She added a guileless, "After I've met with Adam's lawyer."

Perine had hooded eyes that gave away little, tight knots of salt-and-pepper hair and a square body that reminded her of trainers she'd seen at the gym where Adam had boxed on his off time.

Polished through practice was Maya's take on the man. But the words *shrewd*, *devious* and *ruthless* also sprang to mind. If she'd been Gene McGraw, she wouldn't have been trailing him so overtly around the city.

Then again, Nathan Hammond had done it and survived. So, apparently, had Captain Drake. Which suggested she could add *slippery* and *prudent* to her list of adjectives.

She nudged Tal's arm. "Can we go now?"

"Yeah, we can go." He hadn't really taken his eyes off Perine since they'd arrived at his table. He'd also left a portion of the gun he'd stuck in his waistband showing.

Although clearly McGraw wanted to stay, at a head motion from Tal, he spun on his heel and stalked off.

"We could have charged that lackey of his with attempted abduction and pissed Perine off royally in the process," the detective grumbled several strides later.

"He was plenty pissed off already." Tal stuffed his gun fully out of sight. "Are you sure you're okay?" he asked Maya.

"I'm fine. He didn't hurt me, and despite what you both believe, I don't think he was carrying a weapon."

"You don't think," McGraw countered. "But then weapons are easily ditched, aren't they? You two coming or not?"

Maya slowed, waved a hand in front of her face. "Actually, I feel a bit faint after my ordeal. A nice rumba might steady me."

The detective snorted. "Rum maybe. Three fingers, straight up." He pursed his lips. "Actually, that's not a bad idea." McGraw made for the bar.

"I saw it." Tal watched McGraw make his way to the bar. "Perine's fists wanted to clench three times. Once when I asked about the Ricolini Brothers."

"A second time when Nate Hammond's name came up." Maya smiled serenely. "And again when I reminded him that I was the last person to see Adam alive."

"Subtle innuendos, Doc."

"Worked, didn't it?"

Keeping his eyes on her face, Tal brought her fingers to his lips. "A rumba, huh?"

"The Girl from Ipanema" flowed through the club's speakers. Maya grinned. "This is a samba, but—and please don't tell anyone in my family I said so—they're the same thing to most people."

"Either one feels like trouble to me."

"If you're looking for it." She shimmied closer. "We danced at my wedding reception, Lieutenant. Don't know if you remember or not." She certainly did. "It was only the second time we'd met."

Those amazing eyes held hers. "The first was at the hospital. You were a resident, making rounds in the E.R."

"Thought that night might stick. You had a knife wound. Left shoulder." She traced the line from memory, ran a light finger over his jacket. "You were a little green that evening, Tal. Because of the blood, I thought at first. Then I realized it was the needle."

"No needle intended for use on humans should be that big. I thought I'd been admitted to a veterinary clinic by mistake. One look at that syringe would have turned a horse green."

She caught him by the lapels, drew him toward her. "McVey handled it well enough."

"Is McVey a horse?"

"No, a man. Tall, very thin, a bit jaundiced. He does odd jobs at a low-rent apartment complex."

"My guess is he does more than that if he can take one of your shots without flinching."

"Oh, he flinched. He just didn't coil up and hiss."

A smile tugged at Tal's lips as she eased him onto the dance floor. "I don't hiss, Maya."

But he coiled up. He also kept his distance and very seldom let his guard drop even an inch. Maya knew something in his past had caused him to erect that wall; she just didn't know what. Not entirely. Since they'd met, he'd remained on one side and kept her firmly on the other.

The laser ribbons softened to a silvery glow, like starlight and moonbeams on a hot summer night. Maya felt the glamour of another era slide through her. No mad pace, no pressure, no killer lurking in the corner booth. It was just Tal and her and a sensuous Latin rhythm.

"Relax, Lieutenant." She moved into his arms. "I said I wanted to dance, not make out on the dance floor."

Mere inches away, Tal's eyes mesmerized her. "Have I mentioned the word *trouble* at all?"

"Mentioned, yes. Didn't explain why."

"You know why, Maya."

She could have played the game, but it really wasn't her style. So she hooked her arms around his neck, tipped her head back and met his gaze.

"You scared me that night in the E.R., Lieutenant Talbot."

Setting his hands on her hips, he eased her into him. "No more than you scared me—from hospital to wedding reception to poker nights to beach barbecues. You were Adam's wife and off-limits. Tempting, but forbidden, because Adam was my friend."

"And after we divorced? Was I still off-limits then?"

"For me, yes." His gaze dropped, just for a second, to her mouth. "Not for the same reason, but you were still untouchable."

A sigh of frustration gathered at her throat, but rather

than give in to it, she moved her hips against him. "That sounded suspiciously close to a hiss, Lieutenant." Regret moved in. "Tal, why did we let go of something that could have been so good?"

His lips brushed her cheek, turned a light shiver into a fiery tug of desire. "It isn't always about what we want. For me, it's about knowing who I am, where I come from, what I'm capable of."

Despite his ominous tone, Maya wasn't buying. She'd heard stories from Adam, some of them conjecture, most of them not, of an embittered mother and a father who'd faded to black early in Tal's childhood. As hers—minus the bitter mother—had done.

Because she knew he wouldn't, she lifted her mouth, took his lower lip between her teeth and nipped. "You're going to tell me you have a temper, but I already know that. Tempers don't scare me, Tal. My mother was Venezuelan. I grew up immersed in the Latin temperament. Very vocal, very demonstrative, very short on fuse."

"Maya "

She felt his resistance melting and nipped again. "Why don't you try kissing me instead of shoring up that wall of yours?"

"I could hurt you."

Her arms tightened around his neck. "Take your best shot, Lieutenant."

Chapter Six

He should have given her details. Should have pulled her off the dance floor and out of the club. But he hadn't, and then she'd kissed him. More disturbing, he'd kissed her back. He'd practically devoured her—until instinct had kicked in and sanity had returned. If you could call his behavior sane.

He'd driven her home, dropped her off, made sure her guards were in position. Then he'd left, with guilt and frustration boiling like lava in his gut.

Now the bedside clock ticked in his brain, and of course, the nightmares returned full force. There were shouts and screams and doors being slammed. Tires squealed on wet pavement. His mother snared his wrist, hauled him into the light, forced him to look at the bruises.

"He's in you, Stephen," she whispered. "Jekyll and Hyde, living inside you. But you know Hyde won't stay hidden forever. He can't. He's too strong, too cruel, too much a part of what you are...."

Tal shot upright in his bed as her voice trailed away. Breathing hard, he swore through clenched teeth. Through clenched stomach and neck muscles and, most telling of all, through clenched fists.

He didn't punch the nearest wall, as he would have liked. Instead, he fell back on the mattress and waited it out. He simply stared at the ceiling and watched the harbor lights create grotesque patterns on it.

He'd been houseboat sitting off and on for the past eighteen months. Friend of a friend of a friend. He had no idea who the owner was. Hell, it could be Perine, for all he knew.

As the nightmare receded, he let his eyes close and his mind drift. No surprise it drifted straight to Maya But then, what did he expect at this point?

Yeah, okay, he'd turned green the night they'd met. Who wouldn't? Driscoll had had the look of a mad scientist in that E.R. ward. While seven residents watched, he'd shown them how to administer a tetanus booster, one agonizing step at a time.

"Sadist bastard." Although he clearly recalled the licks of pain, Tal's lips curved. Okay, so the local hadn't been totally effective. One look at Maya, and no way was he going to complain. He'd sucked it up, taken the shot and hoped like hell he wouldn't pass out. Couldn't impress anyone that way.

Then Adam had walked in….

Deep in the bowels of the houseboat, the phone rang. Since it was still shy of dawn on a Sunday morning, Tal couldn't see this being good.

He had to hunt to find the handset, finally located it inside the fridge. How many beers had he gone through last night? Four? Five? And a greasy take-out pizza. No wonder the nightmares had returned.

He glanced at the call display as he approached the counter.

"What is it, McGraw?"

"I need a favor."

Tal almost laughed. "You've got to be joking."

"Would a joker be asking at five o'clock on a Sunday morning?"

"What do you want, Gene?"

"To search the Mustang."

"Why?"

"Because I'm better than the people Drake assigned to the job. I talked to him last night. He says it's your call."

Tal examined the dregs in the coffeepot. "Go ahead and search. Just don't scratch it."

"I know how to go through a vehicle, Lieutenant."

"Yeah, I've heard."

"If that sarcastic tone refers to a certain fifty-nine Ford truck two years ago, I didn't have the keys, and the guy was a dealer. He deserved it. Speaking of trucks, have you seen Drake's? I'd trade a year of raunchy sex to own that baby."

Tal dumped the stale coffee. "Appreciate the picture, McGraw. One nick, and you're a dead man."

"I'll run it over to your place when I'm done." The detective waited, then asked, "Wanna give me a clue?"

"About how to drive or how to get here?"

"You're pissing me off, Talbot."

"That was the point," Tal murmured. "I'm on the *Calypso Rogue*. It's a houseboat, moored two miles south of Eden Bay."

"Handy to be close to a hospital with such an appealing E.R."

"No nicks," Tal warned and disconnected.

He picked up the key ring Maya had given him, hung it over the kitchen windowsill and turned away. Then he paused, backtracked and narrowed his eyes at the trio of dangling keys.

Why three? A 1967 Shelby Mustang only needed two—for the ignition and trunk. He recognized those right off. The third was smaller, more worn than the other two—and might or might not have anything to do with the car.

Hoisting himself onto the counter, Tal set the coffee machine on brew, held the worn key up to the early morning light and speculated.

"YOU'RE LATE." JAMIE RUSHED to meet Maya halfway down the beachside stairs.

"I had an emerg—" She broke off as her friend and coach all but tore her arm from its socket. "Uh, that's my setting hand you're pulling off, Jamie. I won't be much use to the team without it."

"The first game's already started." Jamie inspected her top to bottom. "What kind of emergency? Hospital or personal?"

"One of my cousins. I can't explain in five seconds. She's fine now."

"In that case—" Jamie pointed to the nearest cabana "—go get changed. You've got two minutes." She peered over Maya's shoulder. "Did you bring your bodyguards?"

"Like I had a choice. They're here somewhere, inconspicuous and, hopefully, incognito. If he hasn't already, Tal will probably show up as well." She snatched her hand away. "Jamie, a shoulder socket can withstand only so much pressure."

"We're down to ninety seconds."

"I'm wearing my bathing suit."

"Bless you, dear Doctor."

Maya managed a smile. "Okay. I get that this is really important to you."

"What can I say? I'm a highly competitive person." Jamie butted her fingernails. "I also have a shot at an intercity coaching job. The extra money will help me put my kid in that much-needed private program. And if I hear the words *borrow* or *lend* come out of your mouth, I swear, I'll rip both of your arms from their sockets." She pointed again. "Cabana, now. Sixty seconds."

Maya gave up. It was easier to let herself be bull-dozed into a beachfront changing room than to have an argument with a nearly six-foot-tall steamroller.

Sixty seconds until serve didn't leave her with much time to think. Probably better that way, Maya decided. Her thoughts would turn to Tal and only confuse her more.

Somehow she'd known the moment she'd seen him seven years ago that he was trouble, in uppercase letters. An engaged resident with a wedding pending and a ter-minally ill mother who adored her future son-in-law had no business feeling like that. It couldn't be real, had to be lust, she'd told herself. Whatever it was, it would go away.

But it hadn't. It had faded, yes, to a manageable level, until she'd seen him again at the reception. God, she'd only just taken her vows, was about to take off on her honeymoon....

"Okay, stop," she ordered herself now. The past was done. There was nothing to be gained by rehashing it. You couldn't unmake a mistake; you could only learn from it.

Oh, great. Now she sounded like Jamie. Do what needed to be done. Let the chips fall.

Except when it came to beach volleyball.

Tal would show today. He wouldn't have the decency

to stay out of sight. He'd be right there, on the sidelines, and one look in his direction would send her setting ability straight to hell. Then she'd have a guilt trip for ruining Jamie's day.

Maya got ready quickly. Expelling a deep breath, she swiped the curtain aside.

And slammed head-on into a black wall.

TAL ARRIVED IN TIME to spot a familiar face. He sent Nate Hammond a lazy smile. "Since when did you become a fan of beach volleyball?"

"Since you told me about your run-in with my nemesis last night." The wrinkles that fanned out from Nate's eyes deepened as he searched the area for shade and finally zeroed in on a palm grove ahead.

Despite forty years in Florida, his New York accent hadn't faded one bit. And nothing could dull his sharp brain, which had never quite managed to retire.

A fit sixty-four, he fished when he chose, sailed when he could and kept in touch with four ex-wives. More than anyone in the department, Nathan Hammond had mentored Tal, taking him from a green-as-grass rookie to his last promotion four years ago.

Together with Drake, he'd also trailed Orlando Perine from one end of Miami to the other.

Tal leaned back on his elbows, stretched out next to his friend under a lush spread of coconut palms and scanned the crowd. "You'll have to let it go at some point, Nate. Leave the Perine investigation to the next generation. If the guy's gettable, we'll get him, for fraud and murder."

The older man set his jaw. "He killed one of ours, Tal. I don't want back in all the way—too many cobwebs in the attic now for that. I just want to watch him fall. I swear to God, he contributed to my partner's death seventeen years ago. Coronary, the doctors said. But Perine factored in there somewhere. We chased that son of a bitch in circles the month before Rayburn died. Hardly slept, lived on coffee, smokes and whiskey, and we still couldn't pin him down. Not him and not the scum on his payroll."

"Meaning cops?"

"You don't believe me, do you?"

"About some of it, yeah. About Drake, no."

"Did you check out the new truck?"

"I asked some questions."

"And?"

Tal kept his sun-shielded eyes on the water, where half a hundred boats zipped, glided and sliced through his line of vision. "He won it in a raffle. Bought three tickets at a booth in a shopping mall. One of them came through."

"Good."

"You're not disappointed?"

Nate snorted. "What? That a cop I respected as much as I sometimes hated is clean? Give me some credit for loyalty, Tal. One of ours, remember?" His gravelly voice gentled. "You wanna talk about Adam?"

"No."

"Thought not. You change your mind, me and my thermos are available." Reaching over, he drew two cans of beer with holders from a worn police pack. "Meanwhile, we can quench our thirst and ogle at the same time."

Tal accepted the ice-cold can of beer and only spotted Maya because he turned his head at the precise moment a man in black shoved her into one of the beach cabanas.

"TAL, DON'T. IT'S MCVEY!" Maya planted herself between police and patient. "It's McVey," she repeated. "Back off, all of you."

McVey shrank into the corner, head bowed, eyes glued to the sand.

Tal regarded him for a moment, then put his gun away and motioned to the men in jeans and muscle tops behind him. "I'll handle this."

The officers left. Only Tal remained, and an older man, whom Maya recognized as Nathan Hammond.

"He's a patient," she reaffirmed at Tal's skeptical stare. "From the hospital. It's okay," she said to McVey. "Tal only looks like he wants to bite your head off. He's really a nice guy." Smiling, she extended her hand to the older man. "Hello, I'm Maya Santino."

A grin took Nate's features from city cop to someone's grandfather. "Pleased to meet you, Doc. Nathan Hammond. Nate. I was sorrier than you can know to hear about Adam."

"Thank you. Tal, stop glaring at McVey." She gave his shin a light kick. "He came down here because one of the E.R. nurses told him where I was. Someone who shouldn't have wrapped his arm last night, and it started to swell."

"And the E.R. nurse couldn't fix that?" asked Tal.

"I wanted the doc." McVey nodded toward Maya. "Don't trust anyone else."

"So you see," Maya said sweetly, "it was simply another misunderstanding."

Nate placed a hand on his heart. "Racing like a subway train. Respiration's up, too. I can't take this kind of excitement anymore, Tal."

McVey stood but refused to look at either man.

"I'll go now. Sorry for the fuss, Dr. Santino, but thanks for the help."

"No problem." She peered up into his face. "Do you want me to call a taxi?"

McVey darted Tal a quick look before parting the curtain. "Thanks, but I'll thumb…walk," he amended and slipped outside.

Maya brought her hands together. "Well, that was a pleasant scene." A shout beyond the curtain diverted her from the subject of McVey. "Oh, God, here we go."

Jamie blew in and snagged Maya's elbow. "Game's in progress, gentlemen. I need my star setter."

"Needs her setter," Maya repeated. She saw Tal inspecting the cabana, and before Jamie could yank her out, she tapped his shoulder. "I'll change at the hotel when we're done. Will that help?"

The near smile certainly did. Helped her, anyway. "Might," he agreed. Then he made her brain blank out when he curled his fingers around her nape and hauled her up against him for a deep and hungry kiss.

"We did it! We did it! We did it!" Jamie did a booty dance from the white sand beach to the luxury hotel. "We beat the Generals, raised some moola for the new children's wing and garnered me a little citywide attention."

She'd prearranged use of the hotel facilities for her team. Thirty minutes and a great deal of shampoo, shower gel and body creams later, Maya repacked her belongings, fastened her pack and went to find Tal.

"That was some steamy kiss the lieutenant laid on you before the game," Jamie teased, following on her heels. Still on a winning high, she gave Maya a sideways shoulder bop. "I didn't realize you knew him quite so well."

Maya popped a pair of sunglasses on top of her head. "No comment, Nurse Hazell."

"He was Adam's friend, right?"

"Still no comment."

"You're driving me nuts, but fine. New topic. I think I'm going to call that other cop."

"McGraw? I don't know, Jamie. I hear he has a nasty ex."

"Makes us comrades."

Maya laughed. "Your life, your choice. But now I need to get out of here, before Tal gets worried."

"There's an exit along here." Jamie indicated a curvy hallway to their left. "I worked at this hotel to put myself through nursing school. Different owners back then, same manager. Do you have Mace?"

Maya grinned. "No, but I have three cops. Four if you count Nate Hammond."

"I didn't notice any cops in the shower, and I don't see any in this corridor. You need Mace or bear spray or both. I have…" She went to dig in her bag and frowned. "Crap, I must have left my purse in the room. Wait here. I'll get it. Mace is good," she shouted, jogging away. "Gun's better still."

"Guns put holes in people," Maya retorted in her wake. But she appreciated the concern.

A glance at her watch told her it was approaching 7:00 p.m. Wherever home was, she hoped McVey had gotten there safely. Poor man. He'd wanted medical attention, and four cops had descended on him.

Running into him today had tweaked the familiarity chord in her head. Something about him continued to ring muted bells.

Not important, she reminded herself. At least not relevant to a man called Falcon or the information he'd apparently given to Adam.

She knew the information was the key. Perine wanted it back; Tal wanted it, period.

Did he want her as well?

Hitching up her pack, she continued along the corridor. She'd promised herself last night, somewhere between the Marbel Club dream and the near-abduction nightmare, that she wouldn't dwell, wouldn't fantasize, would not set herself up for a relationship she wasn't sure she was ready for.

"Focus on career," she said out loud. "Forget men. Forget cops and informants, and sorry, Adam." She sighed as she glanced skyward. "Forget even you. I want simple, and—oh, hell." She blew out a weary breath. "I still want Tal."

The hallway took a sharp left turn, toward some obscure side exit. Tal and her police guards would be waiting in the lobby. Jamie was nowhere in sight. Should she turn around or keep going?

It was only a tiny brush of fabric. Maya almost missed it as she switched the heavy pack to her other shoulder.

Her muscles coiled for flight, but before she could run, something rough and musty-smelling came down over her head.

And the hotel hallway went black.

Chapter Seven

Rough hands shoved her up against the wall. A sinewy body held her in place. Pain speared through her shoulder as her arm was wrenched up hard behind her back.

It didn't matter where he'd come from or how he'd managed to sneak up on her. She couldn't budge him, and she was afraid to struggle, for fear of having her arm snapped in two.

As unexpectedly as he'd sprung, her attacker plucked her from the wall, snatched the blanket from her head.

Opportunity.

As she'd been taught, Maya spun clockwise, into his grip. Spike, jab, kick, jam. Every self-defense maneuver she knew streaked through her brain. Fear wanted to scatter them. E.R. training held them in line.

He swore and scrambled to slam her back, to twist the strap of her pack across her shoulders.

The pack hindered her, but it also prevented him from getting a good grip. Using her free arm, she grasped her right wrist with her left hand and plunged an elbow hard into his stomach.

His breath wheezed out in a surprised "Oomph." She snapped the same elbow up under his jaw. The impact knocked his head back and allowed her a glimpse of a prominent Adam's apple.

To her left she heard a door clang open and someone call her name. Then feet pounded in the hallway. Her attacker reared back, looked from side to side, emitted a throaty sound and fled.

She saw Tal first, followed closely by the guards and Nate.

"Go after him," Tal ordered the bodyguards. He gripped her arms, kept her on her feet. "Are you hurt?"

"Just winded." With a few dots sparkling on the edge of her vision. "It was the same guy from the parking lot, Tal. Tall, thin, whippy. Wears a balaclava. Likes to shove his victims into solid surfaces."

"Maya!" Jamie came around the corner at a tripping run. Winded, she pressed a fist to her chest. "Batman and Robin just whizzed past me. Are you all right?"

Maya let her head fall back. "I'm fine. Tired of saying it, but fine all the same."

When Tal checked her eyes for clarity, she made a sound in her throat. "Also tired of repeating myself, Lieutenant. Go."

"I'm fine," Maya repeated. "Go."

Tal hesitated, then gripped his gun. "Watch her, Nate," he said, and took off the way he'd come.

It was like being in a hurricane—a calm center with chaos all around. Leaning against the wall, Maya closed her eyes.

"This cop stuff's too out there, Nate. E.R.'s way more manageable."

"Has its moments." Nate drew a gun, smaller and older than the one he held, from a shin strap. "Take it," he said when Maya hesitated. "I'm not the shot I was back in the day—not even half, truth be told. Do you know how to use it?"

Maya glanced sideways at Jamie. "Maybe."

Nate grinned. "Adam taught you?"

"My mother, actually."

Exasperated, Jamie set a hand on her hip. "Are you serious? That lovely woman taught you how to fire a gun?"

"News flash, people. You grow up in Caracas, you prep for the worst."

Now her friend's foot tapped. "So how come you'll take a gun from him but not from me?"

"Holding's different than carrying," Maya said simply. She switched her attention to Nate. "I don't suppose you saw that guy or recognized anything about him."

"Saw part of an arm." He shrugged. "It wasn't very telling. The first trick Perine teaches his employees is advanced escapism."

Maya pushed off. "Whoever he was, he's not the same guy who grabbed me last night at the Marbel Club."

Exasperation made Jamie's eyes roll. "Someone attacked you in a club?"

"Grabbed, not attacked. There's a difference," Maya pointed out.

Nate used the barrel of his gun to scratch behind his ear. "Perine hires different people to do different things. He surrounds himself with big boys. That's protection. He gets the sleeker, faster ones to do the jumping. Uses anyone who can be bought for eyes and ears."

Maya laughed. "Well, I feel better."

"I don't," Jamie said flatly. "I made you come to the game today, even though I knew someone was after you."

Going to the corner, Maya peered around. "I came because I wanted to, Nurse Hazell."

Nate studied his weapon. "If you're worried about Tal, you can put that concern straight back in its box. Lieutenant Talbot handles himself better than anyone I know. Could have been a sharpshooter if he'd wanted to go that route."

"Do you really know how to use that thing?" Jamie demanded.

Maya's smile was faint. "Put it this way. If we were in a Wild West saloon, I could decimate a whiskey bottle at fifty paces."

"After which, every cowboy in the saloon would decimate you." Nate cocked an ear to his right. "Sounds like our side came up empty."

Tal was shoving his gun into the back of his jeans when he turned the corner. "No sign of him. He must know the hotel."

Maya resisted an urge to run over and hug him. "Maybe he has a room here."

Nate's brows went up. "Not a chance, Doc. No way."

"Oh, hell. There's that tone I love so much. The I-hate-to-tell-you-this-but inflection. Let me guess. Orlando Perine owns the hotel, right?"

But Jamie shook her head. "The Freemont Group bought the place three years ago. There was a write-up in all the papers. The building's over a hundred years old."

"Jamie, Perine could own or even be the Freemont Group."

Tal took Nate's gun, trapped Maya's chin, reexamined her eyes. "There is no Freemont Group, Doc. Not anymore. The corporation dissolved when its principal shareholder died last January. At which point, this and five other properties were snapped up."

Maya exhaled. "Let me guess. By Delgato Enterprises, right? President and CEO, Orlando Perine."

THE POLICE SEARCHED BUT found nothing at the hotel. Falcon remained at large; in hiding was the obvious answer. Orlando Perine couldn't be reached, and two extensive searches of Adam's car, home and police locker came up empty.

After an unproductive weekend, Maya met with Adam's lawyer on Monday morning. The woman assured her that her ex-husband's will was unlikely to be challenged.

For the rest of the week, Gene McGraw became a fixture in the E.R. Inasmuch as she ever did, Jamie flirted with him. Maya couldn't tell if he was responding or so fixated on his investigation that a nuclear explosion wouldn't have made an impression.

Through it all, her police bodyguards remained omnipresent. Any closer, and she'd be bumping them with her elbows while she worked.

As for Tal, his emotional wall was back in place. Oh, he came to the hospital, even took her for lunch after her meeting with Adam's lawyer, but he didn't share, he didn't touch and he didn't let her in.

What he did do was phone her early Thursday morning—before sunrise, she realized as she groped for her cell on the nightstand.

He greeted her with a trace of amusement. "You sound sleepy. I thought physicians were early risers."

Maya's bleary eyes focused on the clock radio. "It's four-fifty in the morning. On my day off. After two consecutive twelve-hour shifts. We better be talking coronary or worse for me to be on the phone at this ridiculous hour."

"Not a morning person, huh?"

"I'm ending this conversation, Lieutenant. Bye."

"I need a doctor."

"What? Why?" She pushed at her hair. "Are you hurt?"

"No, it's Miadora."

Confusion mingled with the aftereffects of sleep. "Mia-who?"

"My grandmother."

He had a grandmother? Her brain stalled for a moment in amazement. Tal had always struck her as so disconnected from family.

"What's wrong with her?" she finally asked.

"Old age, mostly. Miadora's upward of ninety, although she won't admit to a day over eighty-two."

"Female prerogative." Swiping a wrist across her cheekbone, Maya went up on one elbow. "Does she have a specific health problem, or are we talking annual physical?"

"She's having trouble walking."

"That could be due to any number of degenerative conditions. I'm guessing she has arthritis. Do you know if it's osteo or rheumatoid?"

"Neither. Her neighbor called me. Said she fell two days ago. All she'll say is that her knee is acting up a bit."

"Not that I'm dragging my feet here, Tal, but doesn't your grandmother have a family physician?"

"Miadora lives on the fringe of the Everglades, in Backup."

Squinting at the clock, Maya calculated. "Is forty minutes good for you?"

"I'll bring coffee," he promised. "I owe you one, Dr. Santino."

He really didn't. However, if he insisted on paying for services rendered, she wanted a sledgehammer.

And one clear swing at his emotional wall.

MAYA HATED TO ADMIT IT, but 1967 Shelby Mustangs had legroom. And totally cool bucket seats. Not a bad-looking body, either, if you were into sleek, black retro vehicles.

Too bad it didn't also have air-conditioning. She fanned her face with her lime-green sun visor and looked over at Tal. "I know it's early, but a little traveling conversation would be nice. You've been preoccupied since you picked me up."

He glanced at her. "I've been preoccupied since Sunday."

"Liked my swimsuit, huh?"

He gave her a distracted smile. Lifting a hip, he produced a small key from the pocket of his jeans. "Do you have any idea what this might open?"

She took it from him, turned it over. "Something old. A locker, maybe. Trunk, cabinet, drawer. Where did you get it?"

"It was on Adam's key ring."

"And you think the key opens the lock to the place that holds the information. I suppose you've eliminated the usual stuff." The look he cast her made her want to revisit an early point in childhood and stick out her tongue. "It was just a question, Lieutenant. Did you try the gas cap on his brother's vintage motorcycle? He borrowed it from time to time. There's also the box where he kept the coin collection his grandfather gave him."

"Covered."

"His sister's mailbox?"

"And both garage doors."

"What about that World War II trunk of his father's, which he refused to part with? Got that, too, huh? Well, I'm stumped."

"Keep thinking, okay?"

"Do my best."

A mile of blurred trees whizzed past. Lips quirked, Tal motioned to the glove box. "There are discs inside if you want a distraction from the scenery."

That depended on the scenery he meant. Outside was a little monotonous. Inside, not so much.

Not going there, she decided and opened the box. The stack of downloaded discs had amusement rising. "Looks like we have a choice, Lieutenant. Northwest grunge or Northwest garage."

"Is there a difference?"

Maya grinned. "To Adam, yes. To you and me, probably not." She drew out one of the cases. "The Dead Wallflowers."

"Sounds uplifting."

"Better than the Great—Something-Somethings. I never could read Adam's writing."

"Says something, coming from a doctor."

She refused to smile. "Let's go with the Dead Wallflowers."

"Are all the discs downloads?"

"Would you pay retail for something someone recorded in their garage?"

She saw the humor on his mouth in profile, and after a few moments of tinny music, she ventured a curious, "Tal, why didn't I know you had a grandmother?"

"Probably because we never had a conversation that lasted for more than five uninterrupted minutes."

"Translation. Adam tended to be possessive. Or

maybe—" she slid her gaze sideways "—I knew better than to spend five minutes alone with you."

For a moment, his eyes held hers.

"Pothole." She spied it in her peripheral vision.

He swerved, missed it.

"How much farther to Miadora?"

"Twenty minutes. There's a diner a mile ahead if you want more coffee."

"I wouldn't say no." She sat back, sighed, stared through the windshield. "I shouldn't have gotten married. I knew that, but I did it, anyway. I was only twenty-two, and my mother loved him. Maybe I loved him, but I wasn't *in* love with him."

An emotion she couldn't read flitted across Tal's face.

She would have pressed him if she hadn't followed his gaze through the windshield.

Straight ahead, a large black SUV raced toward them at breakneck speed. And it was traveling in their lane.

WE'RE GOING TO CRASH, was all Maya could think.

The SUV, a four-by-four truck with blacked-out windows, swerved as they did, with the obvious intention of ramming them.

Maya braced herself and prayed, but she didn't close her eyes. If she was going to die, she wanted to see what had killed her.

Thankfully, Tal knew how to defend against such an assault. He waited until the last second, then spun the Mustang into a 180 turn, which threw it out of the oncoming driver's path half a heartbeat before impact.

Suddenly, Tal was the pursuer, on the tail of the fleeing driver, who had a kamikaze attitude and steel body construction to back him up.

Maya clamped a steadying hand to the dash as they squealed around a battered car.

"Being a physician, Tal, I'd like to point out that this chase could put innocent people in the hospital."

"I know how to avoid a collision, Maya."

"Great. Can the maniac in front of us make that same claim?" She ground her teeth as the SUV came within inches of sideswiping a sedan. "This isn't worth the risk, Lieutenant."

Whether he was listening or not, her point became moot when the sedan's driver stood on his brakes and wound up stretched across the road directly in front of them.

Nothing to be done after that except watch the four-by-four fishtail out of sight. And hope it slowed down.

Tal was on the phone immediately—to the highway patrol, Maya assumed. She jumped from the car before he could stop her and ran to the sedan. One of the occupants had a hand pressed to her forehead.

"I'm not hurt," the passenger, a woman in her late seventies, assured her. "I was sleeping, and suddenly, Roy here was shouting for me to hold on." She patted her chest. "I can't imagine why John Robert would be driving like that—unless he's having one of his spells."

"Spells?" Maya took the woman's pulse. It was fast but regular.

"He takes insulin injections. Gets dizzy sometimes. Unless it was his thyroid. Oh, and he also has high blood pressure."

"How old is John Robert?"

"Oh, he'd be ninety if he's a day."

But Maya would bet he hadn't been at the wheel of

his truck. "Have you ever seen him drive like that before?" she asked.

"Haven't seen him drive at all for five years. Still, his sons keep all his vehicles tip-top shape."

Tal appeared, and together, they spent twenty minutes with the recovering pair.

Yes, it was John Robert's truck. They were certain of that, because the front fender had a fence-post-sized dent, and two of the wheel rims didn't match.

John Robert lived in a tiny community called Captain's Landing, population thirty-seven in a good year. This year being not so good, it was only twenty-nine. The couple knew this because they had a vegetable farm five miles north of Captain's Landing.

Since there was little she could do after the woman and her husband drove off, Maya hoisted herself onto the hood of Tal's car, listened to the crickets chirp and the police compare notes.

Fifteen minutes later, she watched Tal walk toward her.

"I've seen your happy face, Lieutenant, and you're not wearing it. Don't tell me John Robert has a history of running people off the road."

"One of the troopers drove out to his place, Maya."

A feeling of dread crept in. "Oh, God, please don't tell me he's dead." But he was. And she could tell by the dark glitter in Tal's eyes, the cause hadn't been natural.

"Whoever did it tried to make it look as though he'd fallen and hit his head. But the wound was on the wrong side of his skull."

She heaved out a breath. "Any suspects?"

"A couple of guys who live deep in the swamp. The Bestor boys. Probably have a still or grow op. Troopers'll check them out."

"But you don't think they're behind it."

"If I did, I'd check them out myself."

"There were no license plates," she recalled. "Front or back. Don't know why I noticed that, but I did…" She glanced in the direction of Captain's Landing and couldn't stop herself from visualizing the murder scene. "He didn't suffer, did he?"

Cupping her cheek, Tal kissed her. "The trooper said it was a single hard blow."

Sliding from the car, Maya dusted off, glanced north again. "Perine?"

"Seems like."

"Which begs a rather chilling question." She met his unrevealing gaze. "How did he know, Tal? How could Orlando Perine possibly have known where we'd be?"

Chapter Eight

"Okay," Maya clarified as they continued on their interrupted journey. "You're saying that either my phone's tapped, or the person I spoke to at the hospital after you called me this morning is on Perine's payroll."

"Who did you talk to?" Tal asked. "I need a name."

"Cassie Styles. She's a new E.R. nurse."

"Transferred in or recently accredited?"

"Fresh out of nursing school. Her mother's a surgical nurse at General. I left a message with Cassie for Dr. Driscoll."

"What did the message entail?"

"You told me your grandmother lived in a town called Backup, so I mentioned that." Maya turned in her seat. "How many roads other than this one lead to Backup?"

"None."

"Figures. Tal, I still don't see how one of Perine's men could have gotten so far ahead of us that he'd have had time to find a useable truck, murder the owner, then come at us from the opposite direction. The Bestor boys make a lot more sense to me."

They made sense to Tal, too. Unfortunately, the simple answer didn't gel with his gut instinct.

"Captain's Landing's on the main road." He nodded at a tired-looking collection of houses. "All Perine needed was our destination. He ordered his guys to get ahead of us, choose a vehicle and drive."

"Why not just hit us with the vehicle he—or they— drove up in?"

"Because that's not Perine's style. And, yes, there would have been two people involved. One to drive the stolen vehicle and a second to follow or rendezvous in the original."

"Why kill the truck's owner?"

"What? You think Perine would care?"

"He would if the murderer could be identified and connected to him." At his sideways look, Maya curved her lips into a smile. "Got it. Couldn't be connected, because Perine would have thought of that and severed all ties between himself and the killer."

"Disassociation," Tal confirmed. "Nate and Drake insist Perine's a master at it."

"He must pay his employees very well. Or does he hire the petty criminal element to do his vehicular dirty work?"

Tal let a glimmer of humor rise. "Sure you don't want to sign on as a cop? Hours are hell, salary's only fair, but you could make a serious difference on the streets."

"I like to think I'm doing that in my current capacity." She pulled the visor down. "Disassociation, huh? Via a ridiculously convoluted MO."

"Yeah, well, straight shooting's never been Perine's style."

Maya dropped her dark glasses into place as the road curved into the rising sun. "Not alone there, is he,

Lieutenant? A lot of us complicate our lives, even though we know the simple path would make things much more pleasant."

Her tone, somewhere between sly and casual, tempted him to chuckle. An old man was dead, and that bothered the hell out of him. But the old couple in the sedan were safe, and so, for the moment, was Maya.

You could pay people to kill. You could cut ties and carry on with your routine while others did your dirty work. But you could never be sure how it would turn out in the end.

The two-lane road meandered haphazardly northward. Maya spotted the sign first, raised her glasses and pointed. "There's the diner. Coffee, food. I'm hungry, and I want—Tal, watch out! A cat!"

He swung the car to the right, narrowly missed the animal's tail and came to a screeching halt.

"Okay, that was too close." Smiling, Maya patted his leg. "But once again, totally impressive. Two close calls and it's not even eight o'clock. This is as much bad luck as a lot of people have in a month. And I'm not even counting the other stuff that's happened. We're due for a change of fortune, Lieutenant."

He stared at her half-lidded for a moment, then reaching out, slowly drew her toward him.

"What are you doing?" she demanded. But her eyes were beginning to sparkle.

He knew he should slam on the hormonal brakes and reverse. He knew it, but he couldn't. Or wasn't prepared to.

When his mouth danced across hers, he gave himself a moment, then gave in to temptation and deepened the kiss to a more than dangerous level.

A smile grazed his lips. "Good enough change of fortune for you, Doc?"

She fisted his shirt and tugged. "Getting there, Lieutenant." He was sliding his fingers around her neck when he noticed a blur out of his peripheral vision. The cat he'd almost hit hopped onto the hood of the Mustang and strutted to the other side.

Amusement warred with desire. "How are you with superstition, Maya?"

Her lips curved against his mouth. "I avoid walking under ladders."

"And cats?"

"I had one once. It— Why?"

With vague humor cycling through the tangle of lust and emotion in his system, he nodded forward. "Because the one that crossed our path on the road back there was black."

THE CAT WAS A MAMA WITH three eight-week-old kittens. The operator of the diner gave one of them to Maya to pet. Fifteen minutes later she was the delighted owner of a black ball of fur called Raven.

"Pushover," Tal murmured.

"What can I say?" She held the kitten up, kissed its soft head. "I'm a pushover for whiskers."

So was Miadora, she discovered. Tal's grandmother had five stray tabbies, who camped out on her front porch in good weather and slept on her bed in bad.

Miadora sat in a ladder-back chair, stroking two of them, while Tal gathered the tools needed to repair the leaky motorboat that had carried them—barely—to her door.

"Water route's quicker, but the road'll bring you in

most days," the old woman revealed. She flapped a gnarly hand. "Unless a storm drops a cypress or live oak across it."

"The road also requires two extra hours of driving time through ruts that would bottom out more than a few four-by-fours." Tal sent Maya a humorous look before heading down to the dock.

"He worries." Miadora sighed. "Can't imagine why. I've got a reliable phone, and, of course, Cadbury here." She stroked the ears of a beautiful chocolate Lab. "All I have to do is send him to Young Wilson's place, and like a flash, the man's on my doorstep." The shrewdest blue eyes she'd ever seen assessed Maya while she probed the woman's left knee.

Miadora Nightingale—her real name, she insisted—still had most of her own teeth. Her skin resembled crumpled tissue paper. She wore dark jeans, a plaid shirt and a bright splash of red on her lips. Her hair was short and white; her knuckles knobby; her left knee bruised, but not overly swollen.

Evidently, Young Wilson was a bit of an alarmist.

"Did my grandson tell you how old I am?" Miadora asked.

Smiling, Maya unrolled the woman's pant leg. "Does he know?"

"Probably not, but that's because he's respectful. Young Wilson says we're all listed on government Web sites now. Ages, incomes, maybe even favorite colors. Tal could look me up, but he won't, because that's how he is."

"Sweet?"

The old woman snorted. "Kind, yes. Sweet's for suckers. Do you like him?"

Was *like* the word? "I, well, yes, I do, actually. Very much."

"Do you love him?"

Tal may have gotten his amazing eyes from her, but the bluntness was all Miadora.

Sitting back on her heels, Maya waved at one of the large mosquitoes buzzing around the screened-in porch. "If I say no, I'd be lying. If I say yes, I'd be admitting something I'm not ready for. So I'll just tell you that we met seven years ago, right before I got married."

"You'd be the one, then." The old woman beamed. "Thought you were when Tal said he was bringing you up here." Her clear eyes studied Maya's face. "You're a very beautiful woman, but I don't see any vanity. Did you love your mother?"

Maya would have laughed if she hadn't understood the nature of the question and where it might be headed.

"Very much, yes. She died seven years ago."

"Tal's mother died in spirit forty years ago, when she joined the congregation of Reverend—and I use the term loosely—Trewer. The reverend recruited young girls for his self-titled Church of Sinners Redeemed. To shorten a painfully long story, I'll simply say that Trewer conned his female followers into believing that sex with him was the way to redemption. Any other sex was secondary. Oh, he was subtle. Had to be, because he also had male followers, who gave their money as willingly as the females gave their bodies. For a very brief time, Tal's father was one of those males. Shortly after he and my Donnalee met, they ran off together. As it turned out, they were sorely mismatched. Donnalee came to believe she was being punished for leaving the Reverend Trewer's flock. She went—well, I'll be diplomatic—strange in the head."

"I got the impression she was still alive," Maya said when Miadora paused.

"In body, she is. In spirit, as I said, she died decades ago. She left her husband when Tal was five. Claimed her husband hit her. Don't know if that's true or not. She said he would drink with the boys, then come home and use his fists on her. They lived in Kansas back then. He had thoughts of being a farmer. One day, she was with him, and the next, she was calling me from Jackson County."

"Is she still in Florida?"

"Donnalee's not a settler. She moved from town to town, state to state. She claimed she was keeping one step ahead of her ex, but I believe she was really searching for Reverend Trewer. Meanwhile, she dragged Tal from school to school and did her utmost to make him feel guilty for her misfortune. I'd have taken him away if I could've pinned her down long enough to do it."

"And his father?"

"No idea. Could be he drank himself to death. Could be he's still trying. One way or another, Tal never really knew him."

"I didn't know my father, either," Maya murmured. "Simpatico."

"Do you think about him?"

"Not really. After my mother's death, I chose to close that door. Do I sound heartless?"

The old woman shooed a black fly from the table beside her. "There's heart sense and there's good sense. I prefer the latter. Now," she said, taking Maya's face between her fingers and peering into her eyes, "I want you to put those medical tools of yours away and tell me about this rich and powerful man who's doing his level best to kill you."

"MIADORA." JAMIE LET THE name roll off her tongue. "She sounds like a character. Worth the trip if you nix the attempt on your life."

They were sitting on the patio extension off the staff cafeteria at the hospital. Maya hadn't needed to explain the reasons for her trip to Backup, because everyone in the E.R. already knew about it, courtesy of Cassie Styles.

"She's losing her shyness," Jamie remarked. "Job'll do that to you. I was a sweetie when I joined the team fifteen years ago. Now look at me." She dug into her salad. "Back to this near miss in the Glades. It was a local guy's truck, right?"

"A dead local guy." Maya's stomach knotted. "Dead because Orlando Perine is, one, into convoluted scenarios, and two, doesn't want any part of what happened making its way back to him."

"I can't believe anyone could be so cold."

"They're called sociopaths, Jamie."

Her friend scowled. "Whatever they're called, I'll have a word with Cassie about professional discretion. Messages go where they're directed, not to any Tom, Dick or Harry who passes the desk."

"Look, don't be hard on her, okay? She couldn't have known about Perine."

But Jamie had switched to efficient-nurse mode. She folded her arms across her chest. "That's not the point. Calls made to the E.R. stay in the E.R." She got up to go back to work.

"Just leave her head intact, and I'll be satisfied," Maya called after her.

Because she'd taken a late lunch break, she had a corner of the patio all to herself. Tired of her yogurt, and too restless to sit, she took her juice bottle to the gate, unhooked the latch and pushed.

Beds of fragrant red roses hugged the west wall. Far below, the tropical blue water of Eden Bay basked in the afternoon sun. Date palms rustled to the right. Glancing up, she spied a bank of black clouds behind them.

"Where did you come from?" she wondered out loud.

The wind was kicking up, she noticed. It felt good right now, but at the rate the clouds were rolling in, ten more minutes and she'd be wet.

Uncapping her juice, she took a drink, let her mind drift. Naturally, it drifted straight to Tal.

He hadn't known his father. No mystery there, she reflected as the first lick of wind slid across her cheek. But what didn't she know?

Miadora had said the man had been abusive. Had he ever threatened Tal? Hit him? Hurt him? Had his wife's obsession with a creepy reverend excited a monster inside him?

The rim of the cloud bank touched the outer edge of the sun. For a moment, heat blazed. Then, very slowly, it began to recede, until the sunlight vanished and only an eerie swirl of breeze remained.

"Rain's coming, Doc," a passing nurse warned. "Better grab what's left of your lunch and scoot inside."

Taking one last drink, Maya nodded. But before she could close the gate, a man bolted out of the bushes. Behind him, branches cracked and flapped, as if a bull were attempting to smash through from the other side.

The man darted forward. Snagging the latch on the gate, he wrapped his fingers around Maya's arms and tugged. Seconds later, the bull crashed through, spotted them and raised his gun.

"One more step," he shouted, "and I shoot."

"ARE YOU INSANE?"

Captain Drake's face had been redder than the haze that had formed in Tal's head when he came onto the hospital patio to discover Maya and one of her patients being held at gunpoint by Gene McGraw.

"Eden Bay is a hospital." Drake enunciated each syllable. "We don't charge in, guns blazing, threatening to blast our way through a doctor—a doctor, I might add, who happens to be under our rather dubious protection—in order to nail a Peeping Tom."

"He's not a Peeping Tom. He's a patient," Tal said from his position at the filing cabinet in Drake's office. "His name's McVey. He's been coming to the hospital since Maya was in residence. If you're interested," he added, with a shrug for Drake's glare.

"What interests me, Lieutenant Talbot, is the person for whom we've been searching to no avail. Code name, Falcon. Last known sighting, Eden Bay Hospital, moments prior to the death of one Lieutenant Adam Douglas Tyler." Drake snatched a computer photo from his pin board and shook it under McGraw's nose. "We have a detailed description. We have a witness. We have information that could conceivably topple Perine's sleazy empire. And what do you do? You pull your gun and damn near blow our witness doctor's head off."

"As a point of interest," McGraw retorted, "the lieutenant here almost got our witness doctor killed two days ago, while en route to his grandmother's swampland home."

"Don't recall mentioning that trip to you, McGraw." Tal kept his tone even and his eyes on the photo Drake had shoved into his hands. "How did you happen to hear about it?"

McGraw's mouth closed with a snap.

Tal's lips curved. "Figured that."

Drake looked bewildered. "Pardon me for being as thick as Mississippi mud, but what the hell am I missing?" After a moment, light dawned and he rounded on McGraw. "That conversation was between Talbot and me. No record, no report. Start explaining, Detective Sergeant."

When McGraw didn't respond, Tal gave him a faint smile. "One of us has to tell him."

The detective muttered, "Be my guest, Lieutenant."

A small part of Tal wished he could deal with McGraw on his own time. A larger part kept seeing a gun pointed directly at Maya's face. Not meant for her, but loaded, locked and deadly.

"There's a device," he explained, "that's promoted as a hearing aid in the media. Lets you listen in on conversations across a crowded room. It's a hit-and-miss thing, which is probably why it isn't the hottest product on the market. But you have to figure it would work well enough through an office door."

Drake drummed his fingers on the wall. "I've heard about those. Thought they were garbage compared to the high-tech gizmos we've got down in special weapons."

"They are," replied Tal as he rose from his temporary perch. "They're also legal. Doesn't mean I don't want to strangle McGraw for using one, but he has a point about Maya's safety. I screwed up taking her to the Everglades, and the guards who should have been watching her this afternoon were inside, rather than outside, the cafeteria."

"Where she'd ordered them to remain," McGraw pointed out. "That's called an uncooperative witness, Captain."

Tal could have argued on Maya's side. However, as a cop, he stood more on McGraw's this time.

Drake snarled as he paced from desk to door and back. "What have you got for me, Tal? I know you've been going through bars and alleys, as well as some of Perine's businesses. Any of your stick-poking paying off?"

"My informants say the streets are quiet right now."

"Do you believe them?"

"No. The streets are never quiet. The buzz is just too low for us to hear."

"Meaning your snouts are scared."

"More scared of Perine than me." Tal tucked the photo inside his jacket.

Drake sighed. "Keep poking, Tal. We need answers, done the cop way. Means by the book, McGraw. One more screwup, and I'll have you bumped down to traffic patrol."

"Yes, sir." McGraw's smartly executed reply was punctuated by a curled lip as Drake turned away.

With a vague smile, Tal opened the office door. "One of my street sources thinks Perine's put some of his seedier business ventures on hold for the moment. Explains why the buzz is so low. Doesn't get us any closer to Falcon."

Drake tapped a pen on his lips. "Have another talk with Hammond. Pick his brain. He still convinced some of our boys are dirty?"

"More than some," replied Tal. "He figures we should

be questioning the deputy chief at this point, although he thinks the real danger comes from the ranks."

"Nothing like a good dose of paranoia to clear away any lingering traces of trust and complacency." McGraw gave Tal a push through the doorway. "Getting late, Lieutenant. Think I'll check out a few of Perine's less reputable establishments tonight. Care to join me?" With a nod, he all but bulldozed Tal toward the men's room.

He looked left then right as they entered. "Good. Empty."

Hardly surprising since it was after midnight. Tal headed for the sink to wash his hands. "What do you want, Gene? I have better things to do than share a men's room moment with you."

"Drake," was all the detective said.

Tal swiped at the water that had splashed on his fly. Unfortunately, he knew where McGraw was headed. Because, also like McGraw, he'd seen the expensive trinket on Drake's wrist. "It's just a watch…" he began, but the other cop cut him off.

"New watch, Lieutenant."

"It could have been a gift."

"Yeah, and I could have been a five-star general in a perfect world." replied McGraw. A wad of paper towels found its way into Tal's hands. "In this imperfect one, I'm thinking payoff."

Mildly annoyed, Tal tossed the crumpled towels. "Maybe he sold his new truck."

"So he could buy a Tag Heuer, with a whack of fancy doodads he wouldn't have a clue how to use? Try again, Glinda."

Tal started for the door. "I'm meeting someone tonight. I'll look into it when I'm done."

"Does this someone have long, dark hair and a body that makes men's jaws bounce off their beer bellies?"

With his hand on the inner frame, Tal sent him a grin. "I'll tell Hopper he has an admirer."

McGraw made a sound of disgust. "Guy's a crap snitch. Thirty percent at best."

"Interesting you'd know that. I'll check out the watch."

"And if it checks badly?"

Staring McGraw down took several long seconds. Tal suspected the detective backed off only because he wanted to get to the bar.

They parted without another word. However, he couldn't shake the image of the designer watch he'd seen on Drake's left wrist.

Or the airline ticket to Bali not quite hidden from view on the captain's desk.

Chapter Nine

"Excuse me, Dr. Santino. There's a man waiting in your office." Cassie's face was only a shade lighter than her flame-red hair as she pointed backward. "He's awesome."

Could only be Tal. Maya flicked her eyes to the wall clock. Would it be good or bad news at 11:00 p.m.? She handed the nurse a chart. "Tell Dr. Driscoll we sent the guy who ate the French bread upstairs to recupe."

"You treat patients for overeating? No wonder you're run off your feet," a male voice drawled.

Ignoring Cassie's enrapt stare, Maya swung around. "Full moon happening here, Lieutenant. The bread this particular patient ingested was dough primed for its second rising. Which it did, in the boy's stomach. He thought he was going to explode. For a while, so did we." She paused, smiled. "Thank you, Cassie. We're good here."

She thought for a moment that the young woman was going to trip over her feet as she exited.

"Is that…?" Tal made a sideways head motion.

"The messenger herself." Stuffing her hands in the pockets of her lab coat, Maya strolled toward him until they were standing toe-to-toe. "I have a bone to pick with you, Lieutenant."

"About your guards?"

A smile made her eyes sparkle. "I love a perceptive man. They're scaring the neighbors, Tal. Two large men in jackets in August, skulking in bushes and rose beds, tend to attract attention. Not to mention the disruption they're causing at the hospital."

Reaching out, she drew a circle on his chest with her finger. Then she set her tongue on her upper lip and let her hips sway. "I'm off duty in five minutes, Lieutenant Talbot. I'd like to think that when I go home, my neighbors won't be freaking because two members of the Soprano family are lurking around."

A brow went up. "And you want me to…?"

Sliding her hand upward, Maya eased closer. "Make them go away, Tal, or I will." She ran a slow finger along the line of his collarbone. "It may have escaped your notice, but your guards haven't been particularly effective so far. Black Balaclava's still at large. They also missed Perine's henchman at the Marbel Club. And don't tell me they weren't there, because I saw them under the walkway. And God knows when or if I'll ever see McVey again."

With his gaze fixed on hers, Tal trapped her roving hand, brought it to his lips. "What happened yesterday was McGraw's mistake, not the fault of the people guarding you."

"Was McGraw at the beach on Sunday?"

He kissed her knuckles. "What's this really about, Maya?"

"Other than a bizarre shift and a brand-new belief in the power of the moon? Nothing." At his protracted stare, she sighed. "The lawyer wants me to go through Adam's condo ASAP."

"Is that a problem?"

"Have you ever been to Adam's condo? The man was a pack rat."

"So?"

"I'm a neat freak. Not exactly a happy situation."

His eyes glittered. "I'll buy that as part of the problem, Maya, but my cop instinct tells me we haven't reached the heart."

"Okay, fine. You want heart, let's cut right to the beat. I received an invitation today. Handwritten and extremely charming. A certain man wants me to have dinner with him on his yacht. Ringing any bells for you, Lieutenant?"

"Maybe. Did you accept?"

She seesawed her head. "I'm good with yachts, but not so great with setups, which this little soiree feels very much like."

Tal regarded her, half-lidded. "Are we talking real deal here? Perine expects you to have dinner with him, alone, in the middle of the ocean?"

"Mmm, yes and no." Then she relented. "Yes, the dinner involves a cruise around the harbor, but it's a benefit to raise money for some much-needed emergency equipment, both here at the hospital and for the paramedic program. Very exclusive guest list. Perine wants me to give a speech."

"Smart man."

She hooked a finger through his belt loop, pulled him toward her again. "Invitation says I can bring a guest, and I didn't see any addendum excluding members of the police force. So what do you say, Lieutenant?" She lifted her mouth. "Do you want to go fishing with me?"

FALCON FELT LIKE ICHABOD Crane halfway through the Hollow. Every sound made him jump. A fly droning in his ear had him spinning to confront it.

He wasn't into guns; that hadn't been his role within the organization. However, and entirely due to Orlando Perine's experience on the tough Mexican streets, he'd been forced to learn the basics. Otherwise, he really would be Ichabod, waiting for the Horseman to gallop in and lop off his head.

The waiting game continued. *Tick, tock, tick, tock.* His boss's patience had to be running dangerously low. As sequestered as he was, Falcon still picked up on a portion of the buzz. Adam's pretty ex had gone to the Everglades and had almost come back in a pine box.

His palms went clammy at the memory. Could it mean the information had, in fact, been recovered? It meant for sure that the cops didn't have it.

Tick, tock, tick, tock...

His whole system jittered. What to do? Where to go? Hysteria would win if he didn't decide soon. He didn't want to die, but by his own hand would be a thousand times better than by the man's.

A car backfiring outside caused the blood to drain from his face. He checked the front of his pants, closed his eyes, breathed. Prayed.

Then slowly, fearfully picked up the phone.

"SORRY FOR THE MESS, DR. Santino." Nate swept aside old newspapers, chip bags and paper coffee cups. "Tal didn't say he was bringing a beautiful woman by to see me." A twinkle lit his eyes. "Lucky for you, I wasn't in my underwear."

"I see worse than underwear on a typical day. And it's still Maya."

Tucking in his shirt in an absent gesture, Nate shifted his attention to Tal. "What's up? Perine make another snatch attempt in one of his clubs?"

Tal indicated an uncluttered spot on the sofa. Maya took it but shook her head when Nate held up his trusty red thermos.

"Perine's keeping his distance for the moment." He hoisted himself onto a fifties-style kitchen table while Nate poured something, likely whiskey, into two coffee mugs.

"Why the lull?" his friend asked.

Tal flipped absently through a stack of magazines. "Lack of opportunity?"

"Not sure I buy that." The older man drank deeply from his mug. "Thinking, maybe plotting, but Perine's not patient enough to sit back and twiddle his thumbs. My guess is he wants your Falcon as much as he wants Maya here. Two birds, so to speak. Three if you count the stolen information."

"Which no one appears to have," Maya reminded.

"Yes, but he'd see you as being the closest person to it." Nate shrugged. "Last one to see Adam alive. Must be something in what he said, some clue that'll lead to that information."

"You'd think so, wouldn't you, but I've gone over it a hundred times, and I can't see anything."

"Adam was smart, Maya. There's something some-where, a clue of some sort. Course, I've been wrong before. Every time I figured I had Perine backed into a corner, he'd pop up behind me. Harry Houdini he's not, so it's gotta be someone on the inside, or very close to it, greasing those tight spots on his behalf."

Hopping from the table, Tal went to the fridge, opened it and reached inside. "You got any names for us?"

His friend chuckled. "You want me to finger Mc-Graw, don't you?"

"I'm that transparent, huh?" Tal sniffed a carton of milk, then picked up a diet soda and brought it to the sofa. "In case you're thirsty, Doc."

Oh, she was thirsty, just not for soda. Tal had looked incredibly sexy perched on that chrome-and-red table. Given the topic of conversation, she probably shouldn't be stuck on that point, but what could she do? He had that effect on her.

Dropping down onto an orange crate, Nate took another swig from his mug and shook his head. "Could be McGraw's on the take—anything's possible—but I don't see it. Face it, Tal. The guy's so damned obvious. If you were working both sides, would you be obvious?"

Tal moved an easy shoulder. "He wants in to homicide. Everyone in the department knows it. So does his captain. Obvious would be him backing off."

"Not a bad point, but I'm still leaning in another direction."

"Drake?"

"Now you're pissed off."

"Only because McGraw said the same thing."

"And that makes it wrong?"

Tal shrugged. "You don't buy McGraw, and I don't buy Drake."

"You don't want to. There's a difference. There's also the possibility we're all wrong and it's someone a lot lower on the totem pole."

"Give me names, Nate."

The former cop gestured with his mug. "Who's guarding Maya? Carstairs and Dole? Both good men, I agree. Hell, I worked with Carstairs for years, and yet…"

The soda slid cold and fizzy down Maya's throat. "Black Balaclava keeps getting away." She said it softly as she raised her eyes to Tal's face. "Penny for those dark thoughts of yours, Lieutenant."

Nate refilled his mug. "He's thinking Dole has a wee bit of a problem. Like mine." He rapped a knuckle on the empty thermos. "Only a helluva lot more expensive. And potentially dangerous if it got too far out of hand."

"Gambling?" Maya assumed.

Nate gave a rusty laugh. "She makes it sound so innocent, doesn't she?" He roughened his tone. "The word's *gambling*, Maya. Bigger voice, deeper intonation, uglier sound. So far he's lost his house, his wife, his kid."

It didn't sound good, even to an optimist like Maya. Still… "With that kind of problem, wouldn't he have been investigated by I.A.?"

"Yes," Tal said before Nate could speak. "Investigated and cleared. He hasn't placed a bet that anyone knows about for three years. He's got a solid rep within the department."

"He also never denied he had an addiction." Nate toasted the absent cop. "Point in his favor, but still worth a look. Clean on the surface doesn't mean squat in this world. Scuttlebutt is McGraw's captain told your captain to cast a questioning eye in my direction."

Maya looked at him. "Why?"

"I took a long, leisurely cruise around the islands last winter." Nate spread expressive fingers. "Never done it before, which is why I could afford to last winter, but a blip's a blip, and as I've implied so now am I implicated. Meantime, the carousel continues to revolve."

"In an endless circle." Tal passed his mug to the older cop. "The only way to stop it from going on indefinitely will be to switch it up."

Nate shot Tal a hard look. "You be careful. Perine knows the Miami streets. Sure, you got your informants and your crooked cops, but take a good long look at that guy who sells you coffee every morning, or the woman who cuts your hair. Perine's on the board of Eden Bay Hospital, right, Doc?"

"Yes, he is, but—"

"No but. Never a but with Perine. From janitor to nurse to senior surgeon, you look hard. Look hard, look long and look often. Because as sure as I'm sitting here, someone you know is on Orlando Perine's payroll."

"That was just plain creepy," Maya stated as Tal scoped out her courtyard. "How do you stand it?"

"Stand what? The thought that I could be working with a two-headed monster or the state of Nate's home?"

"Both, but mostly the monster. I'll admit, the spy idea's crossed my mind, but Nate was so definite about it, so emphatic. He wouldn't even rule out Dr. Driscoll."

"Your mentor."

"Or himself."

"My mentor."

"Or your captain or Adam's siblings or even the guy at the diner who gave me Raven here." She tickled the kitten's furry chin as she entered her condo. "That's way too conspiracy-theory for me. I want to help people, not suspect everyone I know."

"And so the career switch from doctor to cop dies."

"Tal," she began. Her land phone interrupted and elicited a sigh. "Perfect. You agree to be on call, and what do they do? They call."

He reswept the courtyard. "Be grateful you didn't make it to bed."

It had to be the absurdity of the evening's mix that revived Maya's flagging sense of humor. Either that or mild hysteria was setting in. Whatever the case, she gave Tal a short but satisfying kiss on the mouth before heading for the phone. "Don't move from that spot, Lieutenant. Hello, Maya Santino." She frowned. "Hello? Is someone there?"

Still nothing.

"Okay, this is bad." As Tal joined her, she put the phone on speaker.

And listened to the sound of someone breathing heavily on the other end.

Chapter Ten

Tal wanted to punch something. Or someone.

He punched the desire instead, killed it for Maya's sake. Temper skewed judgment and blotted out thought. Keeping Maya alive required thought, so anger would have to wait.

The heavy breather had been tracked to a phone booth on the waterfront. No help there in terms of ID, but the call had reaffirmed Tal's vow to keep a much closer eye on Maya.

Because he loved her? Yes. He had for years. But mostly because, no matter how things went for him, for them, he wanted her to keep on living. Safely.

Where was a damn fairy godmother when you needed one?

Unfastening his shoulder holster, Tal worked the tension from his neck. The LCD clock on Carl Ruiz's wall read 2:12 a.m.

Maya's neighbor across the courtyard had been more than willing to let a police lieutenant camp out in his living room for the night. Ruiz had no criminal record, and his bosses at the Campanole Office Complex had nothing but praise for the man who babysat their businesses through the night.

Her bedroom light shone low and inviting on the far side. Ten minutes of restless pacing later, Tal was rock hard and tempted to ditch Ruiz's place for a more up close and personal form of protection.

Bad idea given his hang-ups, but far too tantalizing as fantasies went.

His cell rang as Maya passed in front of her partly shuttered bedroom window. He glanced at the call display and smiled.

"You're not supposed to be using the phone," he reminded her. "We've wired you into the system in case Heavy Breather calls back."

"I'm on my cell." She waved it in silhouette, and he heard the amusement in her voice. "So how's the view over there, Lieutenant?"

"Not bad."

"You don't need to be so far away, you know. You could sleep here just as well."

"Somehow I doubt it."

"And that would be bad because?"

"If you talked to Miadora, you know why."

She let out a sigh. "It's wrong, Tal, all of it. How your mother made you feel, what's inside you, what isn't. You're you, not your father or your mother or even your grandparents. My father ran off when I was three. That doesn't mean I'll do the same thing when or if have a child."

He traced her silhouette with his eyes. "You'll have a child, Maya. More than one."

She laughed. "Is that Miadora's prediction, or did you pull the numbers out of a hat?"

He caught a sound in the background, saw her turn toward it.

"Land phone," she said. "Voice mail's got it."

"So do we." Tal punched a code into his BlackBerry, rubbed a tired eye. "It's the hospital."

"I know." Maya listened, then pivoted sharply. "There's a fire at the Eden Bay Marina, Tal. Six boats involved. Multiple injuries."

"I'll be there in thirty seconds," Tal told her. Yet even as he grabbed his jacket, he wondered who might own one or more of those burning boats.

IT WASN'T AS BAD AS IT could have been. Four burn victims, all minor, one sprained ankle, five smoke inhalations, two concussions, various contusions and a waiting room full of costumed partygoers.

On his cell with Drake, Tal left it to the uniformed officers and firefighters to sort through the grumbles. He wanted to connect the incident to Perine, but Maya figured it was just the full moon doing its weird lunar thing at 4:00 a.m.

As the last of the patients was wheeled away, Jamie staggered into the empty treatment room. "I want to go home."

Maya lifted her head, looked around. "Is someone talking to me? All I can see are cuts, bruises and patches of singed skin."

"Very funny. Wanna do a movie night?"

"Any night except Saturday. Perine's hosting that hastily arranged charity dinner on his yacht."

"Heard about it. Driscoll's not impressed. Says it's too last minute for us to applaud."

Maya grinned. "Money's money, Jamie. The more we get, the more new equipment we can buy."

"How can you be so cheerful at this unholy hour? Are you on something?"

"Pure adrenaline." Detaching a panel of X-rays, she slipped them into a file. "Are we done here?"

Jamie's grin had a malicious edge. "I am. You're not. McVey came into the clinic. He says his hand's on fire. Maybe he's having sympathy pains for our partygoers." Her eyes snapped up at a rumbling noise. "Was that thunder that just shook the walls?"

The lights around them flickered several times.

"Talk about your omens." Jamie shivered. "Stay safe, okay?" A lone dimple appeared briefly. "And you could give me the skinny after you and the lieutenant do it."

Maya laughed. "Go home, Jamie. I'll deal with McVey."

The lights popped off, then back on, with a sizzle.

McVey was circling the treatment room when Maya arrived.

"I hate storms." He ran a clammy hand down his pant leg. "Thunder jangles my nerves."

"Which can only mean you didn't grow up in Florida." Maya pulled the folding screen across and directed him onto the table.

McVey took her direction but wouldn't take his eyes off the jittering overhead lights.

"Just think of it as a disco ball," Maya suggested. "We're— Oh my God, McVey, what's this?"

"You said keep it clean."

Grateful for her latex gloves, Maya unwrapped from his hand the filthiest sock she'd ever seen. "This is gross. I said clean the area, as in run water over it whenever possible, not smother it with as much filth and bacteria as a single piece of fabric can hold."

The lights and monitors fluttered. "Power's gonna go," McVey predicted. "What happens when it goes?"

"We'll have to amputate by candlelight."

His Adam's apple bobbed with each nervous swallow. "Is there backup?"

She relented. "Yes, there's backup. More than enough to—"

As if on cue, the treatment room went dark.

"Dr. S.?"

A long three seconds later, the generators kicked in. Maya's lips twitched. "And then there was light."

"More like brown, you ask me."

"O.R.s, life-support systems, monitors, etc. all have full power. The rest of the hospital just gets enough to— Ouch!" She jerked back as his good hand clamped onto her arm. "What is it?"

When he didn't answer, she followed his riveted gaze through the film of brown light to the visible edge of the door. And finally saw what he did. "Oh, damn! Get down!" She fixated on the gun, couldn't see the person wielding it. "Not a sound," she whispered. "Not a movement."

"But..."

"Shh. We're behind a screen. He might not have seen us."

Thunder rumbled outside. Voices in the corridor grew louder.

"Where are you, Dr. Santino?" the intruder whispered. "I know you're here."

Did she recognize the voice? Maya rifled through her memories but came up empty. "Quiet," she mouthed when McVey started to speak.

The power switch was to her left. Thankfully, it was also behind the screen. If she could get to it, she and McVey might be able to slip through the connecting door to treatment room three.

Whether accidentally or not, McVey helped her out by bumping his foot against an IV stand behind him. It rolled several inches, hit the examining table, then wobbled precariously as it endeavored to regain its balance.

As the gun whipped around, Maya ran for the power switch. Before the intruder could orient himself in the full darkness, she snagged McVey's arm. "This way. Very quiet."

On hands and knees, they eased through the door— or started to.

A startled sound from the intruder preceded a shot, which zinged off a metal surface and had a panicky McVey shoving her ahead of him.

"Go, go, go," he pleaded.

If she hadn't moved, Maya suspected he would have leapfrogged over her.

There were thuds and scrapes and crashes, followed by another shot. Screams erupted in the corridor.

"Who's that now?" McVey whispered.

Maya only saw one shadow. She tried to drag Mc-Vey backward. "We have to keep moving." Then she paused and squinted. The shadow had long hair. "Tal?" Her breath rushed out as he joined them. "Thank God."

Tal assumed a protective stance in front of her. "Where's security?"

"Where are your police guards?"

He pushed her and McVey ahead of him.

"Where are we going?" she demanded.

Tal trained his gun on the connecting door. "Nearest exit."

"That'll be the medicine room."

The door between treatment rooms four and three slammed open. Tal aimed but didn't fire. "Keep moving," he said over his shoulder.

Maya shook her head. "Tal, I can't...."

"Get your patient out of here, Maya."

A bullet struck the counter far to her left. Could the shooter see them, or was he firing blind? Working the door open, she propelled McVey forward.

More thunder rumbled as she located another switch, plunging the room into black.

Tal's fingers wrapped around her nape. "Stay here," he said, then gave her a quick kiss and took off.

She heard a shot. A door slammed. McVey flinched but held fast to her arm. His fingers felt like talons digging into her flesh.

"McVey, you're not helping."

"You can't go after him." His grip tightened.

Was it unethical to kick a patient under these circumstances?

She twisted her arm instead and broke his grip.

The main corridor was accessible only through the nurse's station. Maya ran from memory, spotted an outline and barely avoided a head-on collision.

A white-faced Jamie snatched her into a hard hug. "There's a guy with a gun."

Maya nodded. "We met."

"I saw the lieutenant."

"Where?"

"Heading for the fire door. He was chasing the gun guy, but he had to keep dodging people, and the gun guy had a long lead."

Planting her hands against her friend's shoulders, Maya shoved herself away. The hazed light made Jamie's features look thin and waxy. "Did you see the guy? His face?"

"No, he had a thing on."

"A balaclava?"

"Okay, sure. He was tall, I saw that. And he had long legs, sort of skinny."

Maya glanced at the fire door. Would it help Tal or hinder him if she followed? Did she need to ask?

A tall, heavyset man staggered into the corridor. Gasping, he pinwheeled his arms. "Help me please!"

"Jamie, bag," Maya ordered.

Her friend backtracked, rummaged.

"You're okay," Maya told the man. "Just breathe." She guided him to a chair, hoped it wouldn't fold under his weight, then set the bag Jamie gave her over his mouth. "Breathe in and out. That's good."

McVey crept forward. "Fish?"

The man's eyes came up. He panted something unintelligible.

McVey raised his voice. "Do what the doctor says, Fish."

"Is that his real name?" Maya asked.

"No, it's just what he's called. Real name's Jimmy Blower. People started calling him Blowfish, then Big Fish. You know, the guy you can see coming a mile away. I guess they figure he's a big fish doing his wheeler-dealer business thing in a little pond."

"THAT'S WHAT HE SAID, Tal. Exactly what he said. "They figure he's a big fish doing his wheeler-dealer business thing in a little pond."

"Which is more or less what Adam said to you before he died. I get it, Maya."

"And?"

"I'll check him out. Jimmy Blower. I'm also going to take a closer look at the vanishing act you call McVey." He frowned, trapped her probing hand. "What are you doing?"

"Checking you out." She opened his jacket, pressed her fingers to his rib cage. "You're soaked and muddy and God knows what else. You also hate needles. The balaclava guy could have stabbed you, but I'm guessing that isn't something you'd share."

He caught her wrists. "He didn't stab me, okay? Didn't stab, didn't shoot, didn't do anything except disappear. Like your cryptic street patient."

"McVey'll turn up. Eventually."

"Convenient as well as cryptic, huh?"

"I don't think he meant to be cryptic. I just thought it was strange that he'd use that particular phrase at this particular time. Or that some guy called Big Fish would show up in the hospital right after someone else shot at me—us."

"You, Maya." Tal ran his thumbs over her knuckles, mesmerized her with his steady stare. "You're the target."

"Fine. I'm the target. Before you ask, the answer's no. I won't hide. I can't. We're short staffed as it is, and I promised Adam I'd handle his legal affairs."

"Are those supposed to be good reasons for risking your life?"

"Best I've got. Besides—" she tugged on her trapped wrists "—if Perine has as many contacts as you and

Nate seem to think, hiding won't do me any good. If there's one slip of the tongue, if good cop accidentally tips bad cop, grocery boy shoots me."

"Or shoots around you."

"Excuse me?" They were standing in the doctor's lounge. However, since there were still people in the corridor outside, she lowered her voice. "Those were real bullets that guy was firing, right?"

"Off the mark, but, yeah, real."

"Last I heard, Tal, real bullets put real holes in people. It put one in Adam."

"Just a thought I'm forming, Maya. A conjecture."

"You think Perine wants me alive? Not that I don't prefer the idea, and I'll agree it makes sense if he thinks I can lead him to the information Falcon gave Adam, but facts are facts, Tal, and bullets do kill."

"If they hit, yes. Otherwise, not so much."

"Okay, that's it." She yanked free. "I'm going home. I've got two days off, and I'm not on call. I'm going to shower, eat and sleep. Then I'm going to force myself to get started on Adam's condo."

She knew he wanted her to back up. When she didn't retreat, he took her face in his hands and eased her up against the door.

Trouble, she thought as a vague smile stole across his lips.

"Have you ever not taken risks, Dr. Santino?"

For a moment Maya simply couldn't speak. She'd never been hypnotized before, but this had to be close to it, because she couldn't take her eyes off him.

Logically, that only left one option. In a single, hungry motion, she fisted her hands in his hair and dragged his mouth onto hers.

Chapter Eleven

There might be no place like home for Dorothy, but Maya liked living over the rainbow. If they'd been in Oz, she'd have lured Tal into the nearest bed. Unfortunately, a doctor's lounge didn't have the same appeal as a field of poppies. And then Tal's cell had beeped....

As frustrated as she'd been, Maya tried for a philosophical approach. When it was right, it would happen.

She managed, wasn't sure how, to sleep until late afternoon. Tal called three times. That improved her mood. At four, he appeared on her doorstep, with two large lattes and a cinnamon Danish. The rainbow returned.

Thirty minutes later, they had an array of boxes, bags and blue bins stuffed in the trunk of the Mustang.

Adam's condo would have had a distant beach view if it had been situated at the front of the building. Sadly, it overlooked a narrow alley, a sea of trash cans and the rear wall of a Portuguese restaurant.

"I'm getting a definite seventies vibe here," Tal remarked as he gave the door a shove with the heel of his hand. "You don't see wallpaper like this every day."

From the threshold, Maya scanned the living room. "If you can see wallpaper, you have a better eye than me.

This is gross. It smells like wet dog fur, and he didn't even own a dog."

She watched him make his way toward the kitchen. "Tal, why did you sleep in your truck when we got back from the hospital? I know Mr. Ruiz's place was out of the running after six in the morning, but you could have used my sofa. I wouldn't have jumped you." Probably wouldn't have, anyway.

The look he shot her felt like hot smoke, the kind that fried lungs. "You jumping me wasn't the problem, Maya."

Point made.

He smiled before he turned away. "I'll flip you for the kitchen. Loser goes in."

She called heads and won.

An hour passed. Although she hadn't asked for help, she was relieved to hear Jamie at the front door.

Twenty minutes later, Nate appeared, with his thermos, two six-packs, a bag of deli sandwiches and the thoughtful addition of a single diet soda. Maya gave him points for pitching in, even though he couldn't find fault with the place.

"Feels lived-in to me," he drawled. Then winked. "Maybe that's why Stella divorced me. Or was it Maddy who liked clean?"

On her knees, outside the hall closet, Maya asked, "How many times have you been married?"

"Four." Nate poured a cup of whiskey, toasted the absent quartet. "All of 'em fair and loving women. Not their fault things didn't work out. The kiss of death for any marriage, pretty Maya, is obsession. I wanted Perine brought down so badly, I sacrificed my life, my relationships and a good portion of my happiness to get him."

"Is that why you want Tal to catch him now? To satisfy your obsession?"

"That's some of it, sure. The rest?" He glanced at the kitchen. "Let's just say, I don't drink so much for pleasure these days as for medicinal purposes." He raised a warning finger. "Not a word, Doc. I've got a right to do this my way, and you've got an oath to uphold. Besides, I haven't told you anything, have I?"

Maya had no idea what to say. Or maybe she did. Dusting her hands along her legs, she regarded him from the floor. "He'd want to know, Nate. He should know."

"He will. Might already. Might have a suspicion, anyway. Two, three months, tops. No cures, no treatment, no way back. And no chance I'm going to let my friends watch me wither. So, I'll tell him, pretty Maya. Just as soon as I see a pair of handcuffs around Orlando Perine's wrists. I'll tell him then. And after I tell him, we'll, all of us, celebrate life."

NATE'S UNDISCLOSED TRUTH haunted Maya throughout the afternoon. As a physician, she was obliged to keep his confidence. As a woman, she wanted to go straight to Tal. As a person, she acknowledged there were times when life sucked.

"Tropical Storm Horace," Jamie called from the living room. She formed her hand into the shape of an arrow. "Heading straight for us. Slow-mo for the moment, but it's gaining strength. Could put a crimp in our onboard charity dinner plans."

"I wouldn't mind being a fly on the wall at that little shindig," Nate remarked. He chuckled when Maya opened her mouth. "Don't say it, Doc. You know a fetching female who'd be happy to indulge an old man?"

"Well, I do—minus the old-man part."

"Maya, if Perine sees me on his yacht, he'll go ballistic."

Tal chuckled in passing. "Might be worth it just for the fireworks display." As Nate returned to scrubbing the bathroom, Tal crouched to inspect a cabinet all but buried under pizza boxes and sticky ice cream cartons.

"Kind of kills your appetite, doesn't it?" Maya went to her knees beside him. "Poke the top left corner, and it'll open. Don't know what'll fall out, but with Adam, that was half the adventure."

Tal nudged aside a stack of boxes. "You're the adventurous one. You poke. I'll watch."

Smiling serenely, she unlatched the door. And saw his brows go up when he spied the stack of magazines inside.

"You're thinking *Playboy*, aren't you?"

"Last I heard, Adam was a guy."

"Uh-huh." She drew out fifty plus Sudoku magazines. "Apparently, I don't want to go through your cupboards." She had to crawl partway inside to access the second stack. "This is called fanaticism, but I can't fault a man who prefers words to breasts."

"Absolutely no comment."

Handing him the last of the magazines, she bent to peer inside. "That's it. Recycle bin. Only Adam would keep…Wait a minute." She stuck her head in deeper. "There's no back on this cabinet. He must have cut it out and fastened the sides to the wall. Or… Ah." Easing out, she snagged his waistband and tugged on the key ring there. "What fits a mini wall safe, Lieutenant? Answer? A mini key."

Tal bent to squint at the safe Adam had rigged behind the battered storage cupboard. "Better than a treasure chest."

"Maybe." Maya tried the key. "Or not. It won't go in."

"Turn it over."

"Thought of that." Switching up for down, Maya was finally able to push the key into the lock. "It's in." She gave it a twist. "It's open." And sliding her hand inside, she drew out a long metal box.

EMOTIONAL LETDOWNS SELDOM fazed Tal. That didn't mean he expected them, but you had to figure the odds had been high at the outset. Simple solutions rarely panned out.

All they'd discovered in the box had been marriage and birth certificates, divorce papers and records of a bank loan paid back three years ago.

If Falcon's information had been there briefly, Adam had taken it out before he'd died. Personally, Tal didn't think the box and the information were connected in any way. The key was either a deliberate red herring— possible but not likely, in his opinion—or it had found its way onto the ring at some past date and had never been removed. Either way, it was a dud.

"This case is a mess." An out-of-sorts Captain Drake reloaded his gun at the practice range. "No surprise since it's never been anything but. Did you connect Perine to that marina fire?" he asked Tal, who stood at his right.

"Nothing to connect. Chef on one of the boats screwed up a flambé. Instant fire. Incompetence added to combustibles, mixed with panic. Three of the six boats were loaded with drunk partyers, and the fire spread. The lawsuits'll go on for months."

"What about Dole?"

Tal eyed his own target. "He's still reading clean. No betting, no gaming, no trips to Vegas in the works." He focused forward. "As bad as it looks, Captain, two men can't form an impenetrable net around Maya in a public venue."

"Especially with God knows who on the take and more than willing to create a diversion."

"Or deflect attention."

"Hammond have any ideas? Damn!" Scowling, Drake inspected his weapon. "Sights must be off. I'm only one-for-five so far."

A ghost of a smile touched Tal's lips. "Maybe you need new contacts."

"Maybe I need a live target. Like, say, a cop killer? Or, better yet, a cop who's playing both sides." He fired with a vengeance, gave a pumped "Yes!" when he nailed the target mid-forehead. "Did you answer me about Hammond?"

"No." And Tal didn't intend to. Not all the way.

"Well?"

Tal one-eyed the left hip, squeezed. "There's nothing. I've talked to Nate, to his informants and to every street contact I have. I even cornered Hopper, and he's got one of the bigger grudges against Perine."

"If someone caused me to lose half a foot, I'd hold a grudge, too."

"You hold a grudge when you lose half a night's sleep."

"Which Perine has forced me to do on numerous occasions over the years. Nate's not the only one who wants that bastard brought down. Why do you think I never made the jump up from captain?"

"I figured you weren't interested."

Drake made a buzzer sound. "Wrong answer, Lieutenant. I spent too many years digging dirt on Perine and people like him and too few brownnosing my way up the ladder."

"Nate was offered that same promotion. Accuse him of brownnosing to his face, and he'll take a swing at you."

"He can try." Drake fired into the target's chest. "I may be losing my hair, but I'm as agile as ever."

Tal bull's-eyed the target in the throat, chest and groin. "I'll make a note, Captain."

"Make an arrest," Drake suggested in a sour tone. "And make it snappy. Before our chief, at the urging of Orlando's new stepdaddy, decides to have us all fired from our posts."

MAYA KNEW TAL WAS RESPONSIBLE for her bodyguards closing ranks to the point of suffocation. They followed her when she went shopping for Perine's charity dinner. In doing so, they also followed Jamie and two other female physicians from the hospital. At this rate, Maya figured she'd be friendless in two weeks. Assuming she lived that long.

They came to Adam's funeral, but then so did Tal and three quarters of the Miami police force. She spotted them at the cemetery, where Adam's ashes were interred. She also saw them at the lawyer's beachfront office, two shirtless men in shorts and flip-flops, skulking and hanging, not even pretending to ogle any of the beautiful women they saw.

Nothing conspicuous there, right?

Adam's final testament was, as promised, short, simple and uncontested by either sibling. Maya handled the details, did her work and struggled with a mounting sense of frustration over the fact that Tal had once again dropped his protective wall into place.

Oh, they talked, and she knew he was watching her as closely as her guards, but touch was nonexistent, and he told her absolutely nothing about the investigation.

"Going to change that," she vowed a mere thirty minutes before the Perine party. Head tipped, she dropped her hands to the bathroom vanity. "Right after I figure out what to do with my hair."

Jamie scooted in from the bedroom. "Leave it down," she ordered. "The humidity will curl it." She gave Maya's strapless white dress a tug, stood back and ran a critical eye over the finished product. "Not bad, Dr. Santino. Your lieutenant will go freaking gaga."

Maya checked her lip gloss. "Thanks for the optimism, but my lieutenant's stubborn as hell and about that communicative right now."

"Tonight may be the night."

Maya debated over a pair of spiky heels, then abandoned caution and went for the look. "Too bad about the yacht. It could have been romantic. Not that the Eden Bay Hotel isn't romantic, but if I didn't know better, I'd swear Tal diverted Hurricane Horace toward the coast so he could avoid a moonlight stroll on the deck… Damn." She sighed. "Why am I doing this to myself, Jamie? Tonight's about money, not romance, moonlight or stubborn cops."

"Just as long as it isn't about dying."

A glimmer of humor appeared. "What, are you expecting Perine to burst out of a cake with a machine gun, ready to blast everyone in the room?"

"Not everyone, Maya, just you. Or, well, maybe that's a bit dramatic."

"Only a bit?"

"Okay, a lot. Anyway, you look too good to die. Truth

be told, you look gorgeous. Now listen up. Your door-bell's ringing, and, no, I'm not coming with you and your hottie lieutenant. I want my own wheels."

Wrap and purse in hand, Maya arched a questioning brow. "No McGraw?"

"I didn't ask him."

"Seriously?" Surprise halted her with a finger on the light switch. "Why not?"

"I thought about it, but then I figured, why should I do all the work? Plus, I think Morales in Podiatry got to him first." Jamie made a slashing motion. "It's not im-portant. There'll be a swarm of police guards in the background, unattached and bored. I like the one with the curly red hair."

Maya smiled. "That would be Officer Dole. I'm told he's a gambler, or was once."

"Match made in heaven. Life's all about risks, right? And finding ways to get past them."

"And then there's watching Gene McGraw get slapped down by a volatile podiatrist."

"Oh, yeah." Jamie's eyes gleamed with malice. "There's that, too."

THE BALLROOM, A SINGLE sweeping staircase down from the main level of the luxury hotel, was incredible. Maya was blown away. But even dripping with imported crystal, fine white china and Thai silk, the surroundings couldn't compare to Tal in a tux.

His dark hair fell over the collar of his shirt and forehead, with just enough curl to make her heart do a quick flip. He was tall and lean and totally hot, off-the-scale gorgeous, in fact, and sexier than any man had a right to be.

He was also about as touchable as the surface of the moon. Or Orlando Perine.

On a stage near a long bank of French doors, the band played a salsa-swing combo that already had several couples up and dancing. From the upper level, Maya stood to the left of the staircase and drank it in, while Tal discussed strategy with the additional musketeers.

Frustration tugged at her. She wanted to samba. She wanted to eat and drink and have fun. She didn't want to think about death and murders, about missing information and possible abduction.

In the corner next to the stage, she spied the man who'd grabbed her at the Marbel Club. Tal had called him Lurch. Maya had expected to call him unemployed. Apparently, Perine's vindictiveness was somewhat exaggerated.

She hadn't seen Jamie since she'd arrived, hadn't seen McGraw at all. She had, however, been warmly greeted by Orlando Perine and his wife, an attractive blonde with a marketing background and a mousy personal assistant trailing along in her wake.

"Wanna bet the mouse has a black belt in one of the martial arts?"

Tal joined her, started to lift a hand, but checked the motion and rested his forearms on the railing instead.

Promising sign, Maya decided, and smiled. "Whatever she has, she's better at blending than those gorillas of Perine's. Speaking of whom, have you seen our host lately? He seems to have vanished over the last twenty minutes."

"Moments after he welcomed the chief of police."

"Who's currently sipping margaritas with the host's wife. Cozy ménage à trois, don't you think?"

She eased sideways, would have rubbed a deliberate

shoulder against his arm if a loud conversation hadn't erupted behind them.

"This is a hospital function, isn't it? Well, my date is a member of the hospital staff."

Maya and Tal turned as one. "And here we go," she murmured. "When all else fails, fall back on bluster. Has McGraw ever tried the subtle approach?"

"Easier to kick a door in than finesse the lock, Maya."

McGraw's voice rose. "Dr. Santino, would you please tell these people to back off and let us in?"

It took ten minutes and two discreet phone calls, but in the end, Maya convinced the security guards to allow both McGraw and Dr. Morales to pass.

While the doctor vented her annoyance to Maya in voluble Spanish, McGraw complained at an equally high level to Tal. He finished with a disagreeable, "I should have come with the E.R. nurse."

In a huff, the doctor marched off. Rather than follow her, Maya accepted a glass of wine from a passing waiter and turned back to McGraw. "So why didn't you come with Jamie? She'd have asked you if you'd given her half a chance."

McGraw's upper lip curled. "I gave her plenty of chances, Doctor. I'd have asked her, in fact, if I hadn't heard her on the phone in the E.R., telling someone she'd see him Saturday night."

"And you know she was talking to a him because?" asked Maya.

"She said she was looking forward to a dance. Unless she prefers dancing with women, I took that to mean she was conversing with a man."

Maya kept her expression light. "Dr. Morales was under the impression you'd been invited tonight."

McGraw glared. "I lied."

Maya smiled. "I gathered."

Tal caught McGraw's arm before he could stalk off. "Coat check's this way, Detective. We'll have a chat while we're there." Sliding a knuckle under Maya's chin, he surprised her with a light kiss on the lips. "Don't even think about ditching the guards."

And go where? she thought, with a glance outside at the blowing palms. Hurricane Horace might be venting the brunt of his fury on the ocean, but even a distant brush with a hurricane was enough to cripple trees and snap overhead wires.

She settled for wandering with her wine and waiting more or less patiently for Tal's return. Or Perine's reappearance.

A man in a white suit, with a blanket stretched across his legs, rolled past in an electric wheelchair. As he neared the elevators, Maya saw an old-fashioned room key drop from under the blanket. Since he seemed oblivious to the loss, she crossed the marble floor to pick it up.

What was it about her and keys lately? she reflected in mild amusement.

When the elevator gave a quiet ding, Maya realized the man was boarding. In an attempt to catch his eye, she held up and dangled the fob. Unfortunately, he was tucking something under his blanket and didn't see her.

She closed her fingers around the key. "Front desk it is."

Turning, she started for the reception desk. Three steps later, she halted, backpedaled, did a disbelieving double take.

A narrow corridor stood next to the elevator bank. The sign above it read Private. But someone had left the door to the corridor open just enough for her sharp eyes to see inside.

Maya wasn't sure why she stepped behind the potted ferns; she simply did it. And, with her fingers wrapped around the forgotten key, she regarded the man and woman who stood outside the door.

The man lifted the woman's hand to his lips, kissed her knuckles, offered a polite bow. The woman straightened her shoulders, smiled and nodded. She turned left, away from the elevators. He went through the door.

Sliding her palm down one of the fern's stalks, Maya digested what she'd just witnessed—Orlando Perine vanishing across the threshold and her friend Jamie walking smartly toward the stairwell.

Chapter Twelve

"It could have been hospital business," Maya maintained from the edge of the dance floor. "Jamie has seniority. She's transferring to the ICU in a few weeks."

"And Perine's what? Planning on being admitted to the ICU at some future date? More likely, he's thinking of having someone else admitted."

"So he took aside a woman who's spent fifteen years as a nurse and asked her if she'd mind shutting down a few of the life-support systems when no one's looking? Can't think why I'm having trouble with that scenario, Lieutenant."

Tal scanned the crowded floor. "Maybe he has the hots for her."

"Oh, come on...." Then she saw the glitter in his eyes and gave his arm a humorous knock. "You're supposed to be cheering me up, not winding me up. What do you really think?"

"Probably the same as you."

"While I seriously doubt that, I'll accept it for now." Giving her hair an enticing shake, she hooked her fingers in his cummerbund. "Detecting's done until after dinner, Lieutenant. No more excuses, no more dragging your feet. I'm tired of being patient and practical. I want to live in the danger zone."

"I hope you mean that strictly in the emotional sense."

She gave his chin a light flick with her fingernail.

"Nothing's more dangerous than standing upright in stiletto heels. However, since I am still on my feet, and before I consume another glass of wine, I believe this samba has our name on it. No more shop talk." When he set a hand on her waist and followed her to the dance floor, she added a teasing, "Although neck nuzzling is definitely allowed."

As they passed the line of French doors, she heard the wind raging outside. But only for a moment. Then it was all music and the magic of the moment. And Tal.

He was hot and gorgeous and quite simply mesmerizing with that sexy, sensual essence that was and always had been uniquely his. She might have lost herself in it if he hadn't lifted his head to murmur, "This isn't why I came tonight."

Easing back, she regarded him through her lashes. "Look, I know you have a lot of ghosts in your past…"

"Yeah, like a temper I don't want to test."

She ran the back of her finger from cheekbone to jaw. "You're a cop, Tal. Your temper gets tested on a daily basis. I've never once seen you lose it."

"I don't want to hurt you, Maya."

"You won't. I'm not sure you could, but even if I'm wrong and there's a cruel streak buried deep inside, I can handle it."

"You don't know—"

She stopped him with a kiss. "I don't have to know. I trust. I believe. You couldn't hurt me if you wanted to. I'm not a victim. I'd walk away. And you'd let me, because no way could you be violent enough to try and stop me. You'd be too busy beating yourself up after the fact."

For a brief moment, he rested his forehead against hers. "You should have been a shrink."

"Right, a shrink whose own father took off before she was old enough to form a memory of his face. I'd have patients psychoanalyzing me."

Lowering his head, he slid his tongue over her ear. "You're not making this any easier."

Heat shimmered in her belly. "Easy's not the point." But then neither was dissolving into a puddle of desire in the middle of a steamy samba.

It could happen, she thought through a thickening haze. One more nibble on her earlobe, a kiss on the pulse point directly below it, and she'd be sorely tempted to shove him down, tear off his tux and make love to him on the dance floor.

Crowd? What crowd? All she could see was Tal. All she could think, feel and breathe was the man whose mouth was making her head swim in fluid circles.

"When you take down an emotional wall, you really take it down, don't you?" she managed.

He knew what she meant. The wall he'd erected around his emotions.

"Consider yourself warned," he murmured against her throat.

She sensed they'd stopped moving somewhere on the shadowy perimeter of the floor. She could barely hear the music above the thrum of blood in her head.

He took his time kissing her lips, parting them with his tongue and sliding deep inside. Maya expected hunger and fire, maybe a hint of reluctance beneath it.

Instead, he explored her mouth with a lazy thoroughness that stripped every thought from her mind.

A purr climbed into her throat. Her breath came faster, deeper. The clothes could go anytime now. So could everyone around them. Leave the music, the champagne mist and the polished floor. Leave Tal's mouth hot and seeking on hers. Leave his hands on her hips and his hard lower body pressed into her thighs. Let the kiss go on and the demons slide away. Let the moment last forever.

"Three wishes," she said against his lips. "Wouldn't it be nice?"

He raised his head just enough to see her. "One's all I need right now."

"That's because you're a man. One word. Three letters. I have several different words in mind, and no single wish could make them all happen."

"Excuse me, Lieutenant." McGraw's sarcastic drawl intruded. "Hate to spoil the mood, but I need a word."

Tal kept his mesmerizing eyes on hers. "Later, Gene."

"Now's better," McGraw insisted. "Perine and his entourage are making their entrance. That would be the usual six-pack of primates, Orlando's lovely new wife, her esteemed deputy daddy, his cop boss and one interesting addition. Can you guess who that might be?"

"Yeah, I can guess." Tal's gaze didn't waver from Maya's. "It would be the owner of a brand-new flatbed truck and a sleek little Tag Heuer watch. Our very own Captain Donald Drake."

"Okay, Maya. Start explaining." Two hours and one twelve-course dinner later, Jamie dragged her friend to an unoccupied corner. "Why is Lieutenant Talbot's captain consorting with the so-called enemy? Drake ate at Perine's table, drank his wine, spooned up his lobster bisque. That's bizarre, right? Did Tal know?"

"Not until Drake showed up. It's a bit of a head-scratcher, that's for sure." Maya smiled, raised her glass as she turned. "So, what's up with you?"

Jamie closed her mouth. "Nothing. Uh, why?"

"I haven't seen much of you tonight."

"I've been, you know, mingling."

"Did you connect with Officer Dole?"

"Who? Oh, no. I saw Detective McGraw, though."

Maya surveyed the sea of exquisite gowns. "He said he thought about asking you to this party."

Her friend's eyes narrowed. "Why?"

"No chance you'll believe he likes you, huh?"

"He likes me, so he came with Dr. Morales."

Moment of truth, Maya decided. "Look, Jamie—" Then she stopped and turned. "Damn, Dr. Driscoll's weaving a path straight for us."

"For you. He never threatens to stomp on my toes at these affairs."

"Don't leave me."

"I've already got blisters, Doc. Have fun."

Inured, Maya set her glass aside, offered the approaching man a smile and vowed that when Tal returned from wherever he'd gone, his own feet weren't going to be any happier than hers.

"WHAT ARE YOU DOING?"

Because McGraw was incapable of sneaking up on anyone, Tal was prepared for the question. Didn't mean he planned to answer it, but it kept the advantage on his side.

"Storm's getting worse." He nodded toward the lobby doors. "Perine might want to think about winding this party down."

"Without making a single snatch attempt on Dr. Santino? Can't see that happening, Lieutenant. Where is he?"

"In the Deco Room. With his apes."

"And our esteemed superiors?"

"Enjoying some of his finest Jamaican rum."

"Now what would be the point of that?" McGraw demanded.

"Good question. I'm running a list of possible answers."

"Where's the doc?"

Although he could see the table where Perine and his party of ten sat, Tal knew better than to trust the situation.

"I put two extra police guards on her."

McGraw snorted. "She know that?"

"Doesn't like it, but, yeah, she knows."

Something flew past the lobby door. McGraw eyed the glass panels. "Was that a tree?"

"Part of one. Like I said, storm's getting worse."

"So we just stand here calmly while roofs and trees and, for all we know, frigging Mary Poppins blow by, and wait for the power to pop, panic to ensue and a certain pretty doctor to possibly wind up with a bullet in her back? Is that the big plan, Lieutenant?"

A hint of a smile crossed Tal's lips. "How long have you been in fraud, Gene?"

"Ten years. Why?"

"Did you ever work under Drake?"

"In a roundabout way." McGraw shrugged. "Mostly it was Hammond who led the charge against Perine and his ilk, but Drake was in vice until five years ago, and the two divisions used to be tight where Orlando was concerned."

"Used to be," Tal repeated. "When did that change?"

"Hasn't really. It's just that if Perine's running illegals, he's keeping a lid on it. There are fatter fish the vice boys can fry at this point, so they're frying them. Homicide wouldn't be involved either if it weren't for those two people Perine offed. And Tyler."

Tal sent him an assessing look. Adam's last words to Maya hissed like an evil north wind through his head. *Big fish, small pond... Don't trust anyone...huge mistake...* "And keys for his condo and car," he recalled, with another glance into the Deco Room.

"Something I missed?" McGraw inquired.

"Maybe we both did."

A large patch of rooftop cartwheeled through the hotel's entranceway. The lights dimmed, then blazed. Tal's gaze went automatically to the staircase. He'd seen this at the hospital, didn't need the sudden fierce sense of déjà vu that swept over him to understand that a repeat performance would be all too easy to engineer under these circumstances.

"Keep an eye on Perine and his musclemen," he told McGraw. "I'm going down."

The fraud cop grumbled but obeyed.

Tal looked for Maya from the top of the stairs. When he couldn't find her, he located Dole's red head and made his way over. "Where is she?"

The cop gestured with his thumb. "Ladies' room. One of 'em. Val Goodwyn's with her."

But even knowing the veteran officer had Maya's back didn't erase the slithering sensation in Tal's gut. If anything, it intensified when the lights dimmed again.

Which washroom had she chosen? There were three in the vicinity. He was scanning the room, trying to decide, when he heard a round of gunshots near the stage.

He swung, searched for the source. And swore when he saw a large, bald man drop to the floor.

"I SHOULD HAVE ASKED HER straight out." Maya pushed through the powder-room door. She raised her eyes as the sconce lights winked. "That can't be good."

"It isn't." Behind her, Officer Goodwyn jabbed a finger. "Neither's that."

Maya saw the Out of Order sign. "There's another bathroom on the other side of the dance floor," she said. "To the left of the bandstand."

The lights blinked off and on again.

Maya looked up. "Second time and counting, Val. How are you with omens?"

The officer squared up. "I say we get back to the main ballroom."

The words were scarcely out of her mouth when the door ahead of them burst open and someone wearing black flew in. A hard slap on the wall, and the room went black as well. Maya heard two thuds, separated by a groan.

A pair of night-lights provided enough illumination for her to make out shapes, but not quite enough for her to evade the hands that snaked out of the darkness to curl around her throat and thrust her up against the papered wall.

"What did your ex say to you?" the man holding her demanded.

"Nothing." Maya had to gasp to breathe. "Only goodbye."

As her eyes adjusted, she saw the outline of his head.

Pale eyes bulged beneath his balaclava. In a sudden, frantic move, he whipped it off, then, before she could react, returned his hand to the most vulnerable part of her windpipe.

"Falcon?" She stared at him.

"Where is it?" He gave her a rough shake. "Tyler must have told you something. I need it back. He'll kill me if he gets it first. Think! Could it be in his condo?"

"No, I went through everything."

"Somewhere else then. What did he say?"

Catching his wrists with her hands, Maya pushed. "I can't breathe."

She heard Officer Goodwyn moan, heard feet in the corridor outside.

Falcon squeezed for a moment, then released her and bolted for the interior door.

Pinpoints of light danced in her head. Maya forced herself to inhale. And again.

Tal ran in first. Hitting the switch, he caught her by the arms. Two of his men went to their knees beside Officer Goodwyn. The rest headed for the second door.

"Are you hurt?" Tal demanded.

She shook her head, gulped air. "I'm fine." Inasmuch as she could, she fought his grip. "Goodwyn's hurt. Let me…" Then memory struck, and she grabbed his wrist. "Tal, it was Falcon."

He tipped her head back. "Are you sure?"

"Yes. He pulled off his balaclava. I saw his face. He's desperate. He must be to have come here tonight with Perine and his army of reapers only a short flight away." She saw a man crouch next to Officer Goodwyn. "Don't move her," she said. "Let me go, Tal." She pushed on his chest. "I need to help her."

One of the officers who'd gone in after Falcon returned to the threshold. "We lost him, Lieutenant. There's an access door in the ceiling. Looks like ductwork above it. It might wind around to the kitchen. Dole's gone in."

Maya saw the expression on Tal's face. "Go," she said. "Get Falcon. I'll help Goodwyn." She held his gaze.

The faintest of smiles grazed his lips. But it was the gleam in his eyes that really struck her.

Anticipation. She'd seen it when he looked at her the first time they'd met, and here it was again. Same gleam, different circumstances.

Part of her almost felt sorry for Adam's informant.

Chapter Thirteen

It was a narrow passage, barely large enough for someone Maya's size to crawl through, let alone a large man. Dole got stuck twice, and the officer in front of him had his tuxedo jacket shredded by protruding bolts.

By the time they reached the kitchen, Tal figured Falcon was probably halfway across the city.

Still, he had to ask. And in asking, he lucked out.

One of the sous-chefs indicated a swinging metal door. The hallway outside, she explained, wound around to the back of the elevators. It also branched off to a number of private dining rooms, most of which were in use. Tal left officers to question the guests while he and Dole continued on to the lobby.

As predicated, the corridor ended at the elevators. Dole turned left; Tal went right. When he emerged, he spied McGraw coming up the stairs from the ballroom.

"Security's watching Perine," the detective revealed. "The bald guy who collapsed in front of the stage is on his way to the hospital. Fainted," he said in disgust. "Explosions were rigged, like I figured, and strictly diversionary, like you figured." He frowned, looked around. "Doc okay?"

"Would I be here if she wasn't?"

"Probably. You'd just be a hundred times madder and a helluva lot meaner. Moving on, who're we after?"

"Guy in black. Tall, string-bean legs. You've seen the circular. It's Falcon."

"What? Here? Why would he—" Comprehension dawned. "Ah, the information. Of course, he'd want it back. Use it as leverage. Clever."

"More risky than clever, but it would give him a weapon and possibly save his life."

"Still, right under Perine's nose?"

"Desperation, McGraw." Catching a movement, Tal whipped his gun around. "There he is. Left of the stairs." But he abandoned the shooter's stance. They couldn't fire across a busy lobby.

Teeth bared, McGraw took off behind him.

Tal would have circled around the wide staircase if a wheelchair hadn't spiraled into his path, teetered on a stuck wheel and rammed McGraw's leg.

"Sorry, sorry," the old man in it apologized even as the wheelchair almost flipped onto its side.

With half an eye on the shadow where Falcon had vanished, Tal replaced the slipping blanket and steadied the wheelchair. McGraw continued on at a limping run.

He was kicking the bottom of a metal door when Tal caught up.

"Frigging bastard got away." He kicked again for emphasis. "Sprayed me with his back wheels and fishtailed around the side of the hotel."

"What's he driving?"

"Chevy Silverado. Big sucker. Older model. Probably stolen. Dull gray paint job. No plates."

McGraw had to shout above the lash of wind and rain. Tal didn't bother to respond. He wanted to get back to Maya, make sure she was really safe.

But he paused for a moment to stare into the storm. Falcon had taken a huge risk coming here tonight, with police at every turn, hotel security, Perine's personal security, and who knew what else.

Questions that had been haunting him for some time resurfaced. After what he'd seen tonight, he suspected the answers might haunt him even more.

FALCON DROVE WITHOUT THOUGHT, without care, and with less than a quarter of his mind on his destination. Of course, the plan hadn't worked. The big man had anticipated him. How? No idea, but he had.

Falcon's teeth chattered. Storm debris was hitting the windshield. He couldn't think. He could only keep his shaking hands on the wheel and his teeth locked together so they wouldn't crack.

What should he do? What was left that he hadn't tried? How many more times could he fail before he wound up with a bullet in his back?

At least he could rule out the horror of torture. Things were heating up much too fast to allow for any pleasure in that area. But he'd still be dead. The big man would see to that. Personally.

Falcon swallowed the bile in his throat. He needed another plan. God help him, he needed to make another phone call. But first and foremost, he needed a drink, a double.

Here's to you and me, Maya Santino. May we both rest in peace.

AS HORROR SHOWS WENT, Perine's party hadn't ended in the usual way.

No one had died or been seriously injured. The man who'd fainted when Falcon's charges had gone off in the ballroom was on his way home. Officer Goodwyn had to be hospitalized for the night, and McGraw had a knob the size of a golf ball on his leg from the wheel-chair collision, but they'd both be fine.

Although she hated to think why, Maya hadn't seen Jamie since their ballroom chat. Almost as puzzling, she hadn't talked to Perine since she'd arrived at the hotel.

"It sounds weird, but I think he was avoiding me," she remarked to Tal as they left the hospital parking lot in his Mustang. "I have to say, though, the few times I spotted him, he struck me as a husband devoted to his new wife."

Tal arched a brow. "Should we run that observation past Jamie?"

"Cynic," she accused.

"Cop," he reminded. His cell phone rang on the dash. "It's Nate." He put the cell on speaker.

"Heard you had some excitement," Nate noted. "Local television stations are awash with speculation. Things settled down now? Is Maya okay?"

"She's with me," Tal told him.

"Hi, Nate," she said.

"Hi, yourself, pretty doc. Talk to me about the gun-shots, Tal."

The traffic light ahead rocked in the gale-force wind. "They were a diversion. Falcon rigged them to keep us busy while he—"

"Went after Maya. Of course." Nate chuckled. "Sorry, Doc. I'm not laughing at the situation, just at the irony of it. It's so typically Perine. Let someone else do the dirty work. Falcon nabs Maya, hoping to retrieve information. Perine nabs Falcon and Maya, kills Falcon, then forces what he can out of Maya in the hopes of locating said information. Once located… Well, we both know the drill, Tal."

"Yeah, we do. Unfortunately."

Maya sat back, ran a restless finger around her bracelet while the two men talked. The background sounds she was hearing on Nate's end had nothing to do with the storm. She suspected bar noise, which, if true, meant he was drinking himself into a coma. It shouldn't surprise her, she supposed, given what he'd told her at Adam's condo.

And there it was again. *Guilt,* flashing in uppercase letters. Guilt at not telling Tal. On one hand, she wasn't Nate's physician. On the other, not being his physician didn't mean she could run to Tal and blurt out what Nate had told her in confidence.

Where was fair, she wondered, when you needed it?

With a sigh, she tuned back in to Tal and Nate's conversation.

"I'll keep you as up to date as I can," Tal promised his friend.

"Good enough." Nate's tone softened. "If you got time, bring the pretty doc over for a barbecue. Poker game's at my place next time. And I want you to solemnly swear you'll gather up your pole and bait on your first free Sunday. We need a Mayberry moment from time to time, Tal. You give him a push, Maya. People on the rise tend to forget that the brain requires downtime in order to function at peak capacity. Case in point, Orlando Perine. He owns and regularly plays on every motorized water toy known to humankind. Rumor has it he's going out for marlin with his new stepfather early next month. If you ask me, I'd say he's doing some pretty heavy sport fishing right there in Miami."

"Big fish, small pond," Maya murmured.

"We've been all over Perine's recent activities," Tal told him. With his eyes sweeping the wet street, he added an even, "You might want to give that flask of yours a rest, Nate."

"Think about it. Stay safe, Lieutenant. Night, Doc."

They drove for several blocks in silence. Maya watched Tal by the dashboard light. He fit the car very well.

She nudged his leg with her foot. "Adam would be happy you're driving his baby. His brother figures you got the only real treasure he had."

"You think?" The look Tal slanted her scorched every thought in her head. Okay, well now she might never think again.

Recovering what she could, she said, "His brother and sister would like some of the stuff from the car."

"Such as?"

She smiled. "Contents of glove box, for starters. That would be maps, CDs and, don't laugh, a couple of old eight-track tapes."

Tal chuckled. "The whole department knows about the eight-tracks, Maya. The car's been searched several times."

"Ouch on Adam's behalf. They'd also like the DVDs in the trunk and the Springsteen-style leather jacket they're wrapped in."

"No problem, but I'm curious about the eight-tracks. Abba?"

"His mother was of the era. The band was part of his youth. For me it was pure salsa at volume ten. We all need our security blankets, Tal, especially in college. Abba was Adam's connection to home."

"And yours was?"

"Nonexistent. I was too busy dissecting pig organs, wearing eau de formaldehyde and sleeping thirty minutes a day to even think about home."

Tal glanced at her. "The scent I remember had nothing to do with formaldehyde."

Those eyes of his should be registered as lethal weapons, Maya reflected. Particularly when turned on the female of the species.

Unfortunately, he had to take them off her at the intersection. Fortunately, the break gave Maya ten whole seconds to restore some kind of order to her jumbled brain.

She caught a glimmer of lights ahead and scanned the darkened buildings around them. "Wait a minute. Why are we driving toward the water?" Then she smiled as the picture formed. "You live on a houseboat, don't you?"

"Why don't I trust that sparkle in your eyes?"

"Because you're a clever cop."

She waited until he parked, then unclicking her seat belt, she dodged the gearshift to land in his lap. Slyness ruled her expression as she unbuttoned his white shirt. "Suggestion, Detective Talbot. How about we use the elements of nature to our advantage and go straight to the good stuff? Say to hell with excuses and let the storm brewing in here match the one out there?"

She saw the conflict between conscience and hunger on his face. In his eyes. In the gleam he tried to disguise.

Should she push, Maya wondered, or let him pull

away? Given half a chance, she felt certain he would, and who knew how high his new wall would be.

"Not going there," she decided aloud and yanked the already loosened tie from his collar.

"Are you having this conversation with yourself or with me?"

Fisting his shirt, Maya took his lip between her teeth and bit. "Pretty reasonable-sounding question from a man whose lap feels like a rock underneath me."

"All because of you."

"Sounds promising, Lieutenant." She planted firm palms on his chest. "How about we try for a different position?"

"How about we do that in a less confined space?"

Maya pulled on a stubborn button. "If you can think that clearly, you're thinking way too much." She wiggled her bottom for effect and smiled when he sucked back a breath. "Now there's the response I want. It says reaction, as opposed to thought." A fingernail scraped across his chin. "Sure you're up for this?"

"Are you insane?"

"Hey, just a question."

One he answered by wrapping the fingers of both hands around her nape and crushing his mouth to hers.

Heat and desire spiked through her, like the bold forks of lightning that had been splitting the sky for the past twenty minutes. When he shifted beneath her, she welcomed the electric jolt that shot from thigh to stomach, marveled at the residual zaps that tingled along her nerve ends.

"Whoa…"

His lips quirked on hers. "'Whoa' as in 'Stop' or 'That was great'?"

"Better than great. I think I saw stars."

"Glad you're catching up. I've been seeing them for years."

This time it was Tal who did the moving. Unwilling to open her eyes, Maya let sensation carry her along. Or maybe it was Tal rearranging her on his lap, kicking the door with his foot, scooping her into his arms while his mouth devoured hers.

The angry slap of wind and rain should have been a deterrent. Instead, it fueled her body and mind.

Desire streaked through her. Warm rain washed over her. The wind whipped her emotions into a frenzy.

Something good was happening here, she acknowledged through that all-too-familiar haze in her head. Tal was carrying her through the storm to his home. And hopefully to his bed.

For a moment, the world rocked. Then, suddenly, the wind was gone, and the rain. All that remained was the night, the raging elements and Tal, whose tongue was doing wicked and fascinating things to her mouth.

Swinging her legs, she got him to set her down. He obliged but didn't release her. And didn't stop kissing her, not even when the floor tilted and her back hit the wall.

That was either the wind pummeling the houseboat or Tal pushing her up against the door. Uncaring, Maya bunched his hair in her hands and kept his mouth fused to hers.

Seven years of frustration exploded between them. Deeply suppressed, cautiously unlocked and now running wild. Running ravenous.

When the floor swayed again, Maya dragged her mouth from his. She took in what air she could, then breathed out in an unbelieving rush, "My God, that was incredible."

"The best is yet to come," Tal said against her brow.

Eager to explore him further, Maya nibbled her way from his jaw to his ear. Opening his shirt, she ran her fingers over his chest, reveled in the tugs of desire that sprang from deep in her belly. "I want to make love, Tal. Now. Floor, stairs, wherever we are, whatever the surface."

"Wood floor," he murmured and threaded his fingers through her hair to hold her steady. She saw the desire in his eyes—anticipation chasing hunger—and was surprised she remembered how to breathe. Could you want someone so much that your motor functions stuttered?

No time like the present to find out, she decided, and grabbing his hair, she yanked his mouth back onto hers.

The tremor inside spread from belly to limbs. She smelled sea air and something beneath it, some dark and sinuous element of the storm.

Tal started to lift her again, but Maya wrapped her legs around his hips. She wanted to ride him this time. Taking his face in her hands, she stared down at him in the murky half-light.

As excitement mingled with desire, she ravaged his mouth, simply dived in and took them both to a higher level.

Her mind spiraled upward, or was that the staircase? She managed between kisses to work off his jacket, left it in a damp heap on one of the treads. When the cummerbund put up a fight, she tore it off.

"Hope this tux isn't a rental, Lieutenant."

"It's worth losing the deposit." He kissed her eyelids closed. "Sorry I don't have candles."

"They'd only be a blur. My head's spinning. Are we still moving?"

"No idea. My brain blanked before we reached the front door."

"Now that," Maya told him, "is the sweetest thing you've said to me all night." Uncurling her legs, she hopped down and tugged at his fly. "My turn now."

She felt his erection and almost tore the pants off. But the zipper finally moved, and she gave it a hard downward yank.

Hissing, he wrapped his fingers around her arms and lifted her off her feet. Once again, the houseboat wall appeared behind her, allowing him to hold her in place for his kiss.

If you could call it a kiss. Maya swore something inside him shot straight to the center of her body. Maybe straight to her soul. Definitely to her heart.

With the next bolt of lightning outside, the wall vanished and a softer surface took its place. Holding himself above her on the bed for a tantalizing moment, Tal ran his eyes over her body.

Maya glanced down, couldn't quite stop the swell of amusement. Exactly when had she lost her dress?

Thought vanished a moment later. Her skin, already warm, burned where his eyes touched it. When he followed the burn with his mouth, her back arched, and her legs locked once again around his hips.

His shirt disappeared while his mouth and tongue discovered her breasts.

When the lace of her bikinis joined it, they were skin to skin. Tal's was sleek and smooth and so beautifully muscled, she wanted to flip him on his back and look at every inch of him. Then he slid his fingers inside her, and the whole room seemed to sizzle.

Her fingernails bit into his shoulders. Pleasure

streaked through her. Had sex ever felt this amazing? Ever zapped the air from her lungs and sent her head into a tailspin?

Not in this lifetime, she decided, then had a moment to catch her breath when he brought his mouth back to hover over hers.

She slid her foot down the back of his leg, ran her finger over a small scar on his collarbone. "I'm loving all of this, Tal. Grant me one of my three wishes, and make it go on forever."

"I'll do my best," he promised and elicited a gasp as his mouth closed on her nipple.

Not fair, she reflected dizzily. But a delicious sensation nonetheless.

She made a purely feline sound, wriggled beneath him. Greedy hands ran over his ribs and down to his hips, then lower, until they closed around the hot, hard length of him.

No walls now. No second thoughts. No regrets. Maya's mind revved. Desire whipped through her, rocked her, almost shocked her with its strength.

Deep breath, rush of need, roar of blood in her ears. Then…

With her eyes half open, she watched his face in the watery light. His pupils had gone large. But there, she spied it. The gleam. Anticipation. Excitement. Hunger. After seven years of waiting.

Her fingers tightened around him. She felt the tiny licks of flame between her legs spear upward. Then he was inside her, and everything around them collided in a wild wave she could only cling to and ride.

It was a rocket flight of color and light. Sensation

after sensation shot through her. She wanted time, just for a moment, to stop.

She wanted Tal not to stop.

Rising to meet him, she matched his rhythm thrust for thrust. She drank in sounds and textures—the shriek of the wind, the feel of his hands bracketing her wrists, the ends of his hair tickling her throat.

The shadows moved, and Tal with them. Maya wanted to pull him in deeper, make it all happen faster. Or slower. Or just again and again and again.

The climax hit with storm force, slamming over her and stealing her breath. The legs around his hips tightened, then went limp. She felt something else now, something like hand-warmed brandy flowing through her veins.

Spent, he collapsed on top of her. "Don't move, Maya. I'm not ready for motion yet."

She inhaled the scent of his skin, uniquely Tal, knew the smile in her voice came out in a lazy slur. She zipped her fingers through his hair, let them rain on his shoulder like a waterfall. "What a flight. No wings. No wind. Only you and me and a sky full of sparkles."

He might have said something back. Her heart was hammering too loud for sound to fully penetrate.

The sparkles dazzled behind her eyelids. Tal was deadweight on top of her. Air would be good, but she didn't want him to move. If she died, at least she'd go with a glorious bang.

She drifted for a while, but not far and not for as long as she would have liked. When the sparkles turned to black spots, she nuzzled his shoulder.

"I think I'm seeing the tunnel," she told him. "Big white light glowing in the distance. Not sure I remember how to breathe, but if I can, I probably should, or it'll be mission accomplished for Falcon and anyone else who might be after me."

Tal took her with him when he rolled away, held her on top of him and stroked the hair from her face. "That whoever will have to go through me to get to you next time, Maya."

She lowered her mouth to his, kissed the corners. "Why are we talking about Perine?"

"We're not." When his lips covered hers, every name, every question, every thought vanished.

She smiled into him. "Wow again, Lieutenant." Staring into his shadowed face, she let her eyes dance. "You're really good at that."

"At diverting the nightmare?"

"My nightmare," she agreed. "Not necessarily your own."

Sliding the fingers of one hand around her nape, he held her gaze. "Forget nightmares, Maya. Right now there's only you and me and about three hours left until sunrise."

"In that case—" Maya tapped a finger on his bottom lip "—we should stop talking and get down to some serious practicing."

"And what would we be practicing, Dr. Santino?"

"Why don't we start with a lesson on how to fend off a frontal attack?" Pushing back, she ran her hands over his chest, then lower and lower. As her fingers closed around him, she bent to whisper in his ear. "Dying to see how you get out of this one, Lieutenant."

Chapter Fourteen

He had an eight by ten picture of his grandmother propped up next to his computer in the living room. Maya thought it was sweet—and sadly informative.

Barefoot and wearing nothing except Tal's Notre Dame T, she prowled the compact main floor. He'd uncorked a bottle of Merlot, but she was more curious than thirsty.

"Do you ever see your mother?" she asked from the window.

He rested his forearms on the galley counter and took a slow sip of wine. "Last time was five years ago. She was living in Little Rock."

"And now?"

"She's not."

"I'm sensing that wall again, Tal."

"My wall has nothing to do with my mother." When her brows winged up, he shrugged. "It's more about my father than my mother. What he was, what I could be. How I might be."

Rather than argue, she asked, "Do you remember anything specific about him?"

"On a personal level, no. She said he abused her. He hit. She ran."

"But eventually she stopped."

"Yeah, when she realized he'd given up, and she only ever stopped for brief periods of time."

"And you're convinced you must be a carbon copy of him." She turned from the windows. "Tal, you can see that's just wrong thinking, can't you?"

"Seeing might be believing to some people, but it isn't always the case. And the seeing's not always true. Deception plays in there."

"So does fear," she noted.

"Thanks for that, Dr. Freud, but I'm not quite as deluded as you think. I don't want to hurt you. It's as simple and as truthful as that."

"Truthful I believe, but trust me, nothing about you is simple. Have you ever looked for him?"

"Nope. You?"

"This isn't about me." At his prolonged stare, she sighed and gave in. "Okay, yes, I sort of looked. Once. I never told my mother, and I didn't put a lot of effort into it. Ultimately, I decided it would be easier for him to find me—if he wanted to."

"There you go. My answer from your lovely lips." Tal swirled his wine. "And so we move on."

As the storm shadows fell away, Maya once again regarded the broody black sky. "You never did tell me how Perine knew we were going to see your grandmother."

He glanced away, let his lips take on an enigmatic curve. "Phone tap."

"Excuse me?" Setting her glass aside with dangerous deliberation, she walked toward him. "You found a tap on my phone, and you didn't tell me?"

"Not your phone, Maya." The smile lingered while he kissed her annoyance down. "Mine."

"How could he do that?" She regarded his land phone as if it were a snake. "Is it gone?"

"The tap? No."

"But that's… No, never mind. You have your reasons. I'm more curious about the how, anyway." Speculating, she pivoted in a slow circle. "Dishes in the sink, laundry hamper brimming, only bread, cheese, two eggs and six bottles of beer in the fridge. You can't have a housekeeper. Even if you did, tapping your line wouldn't be easy. It would be incredibly difficult, in fact. Which begs the obvious question, why yours and not mine?"

"He had to know we'd check your line, Maya, but he might have thought we wouldn't bother with mine. Or if we did, we might not do it right away."

Plunking her elbows on the counter, she pressed on her temples. "Too much to process. I'm getting a headache. Did you check out that guy who came to the hospital the night of the power failure? McVey called him Big Fish."

Tal replaced her fingers with his, but instead of pressing, he drew wonderful, soothing circles. "Jimmy Blower. He seems clean in terms of Perine. He's a bit of a hustler as far as the street population goes. Owns a pawnshop. Some of his merchandise is questionable, but that's not homicide's territory."

"So there's no link to Perine."

Tal grinned. "I didn't say that. Anything's possible. We just can't connect him at this point, and we went in as deep as we could. I'm not as certain of your pal McVey."

Unease stirred, and with it, the urge to defend. "McVey's got a job, Tal. He does odd jobs for an apartment complex. Yes, it's a run-down complex, but the work's legitimate enough." She hoped.

"The work might be legitimate, but McVey isn't."

"Oh, good. Riddles. Let me guess. He's really a high-level dealer in hand-me-downs. Street grunge optional as part of the disguise."

"You paint an interesting picture. Now, do you want the real answer?" he asked.

Frustration gathered. "I don't sense a bad person. Lost maybe, and possibly not employed as he claims, but still a basically decent man."

"He doesn't exist."

"Excuse me?"

"There's no information available on one B. J. Mc-Vey," Tal told her. "The Social Security number he uses belongs, or rather belonged, to a man from Jacksonville who died eight years ago. There's no record of birth to correlate with the information he gave Social Services or his current employer, the owner of a twenty-six-unit apartment building on the fringe of Little San Juan. Cracks and government red tape. People use them all the time, for all kinds of reasons."

Maya sketched a mental map. "Little San Juan's nowhere near Eden Bay Hospital." At a glance from Tal, she deleted. "Okay, irrelevant. Got it. Is it possible McVey or his parents slipped in from, say, South America?"

"We're looking into that. It would help if we could locate him, but he hasn't been back to his halfway house or the apartment building since the brownout."

"Don't you just love a good mystery?"

"When they're solved, yeah. Until then…" Threading his fingers through her hair, he slid his thumbs over her cheekbones. "If you see him, I want you to call me."

"But…"

"Please?"

Her heart sank. "Please isn't fair, Tal. I'm a doctor. McVey's my patient—sort of. I can't turn on him." She squeezed his hands. "What I can do is talk to him, see if he'll go to you voluntarily…Whoa. Wait a minute." She laughed as she suddenly went airborne. "What are you doing?"

"Removing a barrier."

Having swept her neatly over the counter, he pinned her between it and himself. "Storm's moving on, and we're both facing a double shift. But there's always time for one more cup of coffee."

Humor invaded her expression. "You're comparing sex with me to coffee?"

He traced the outline of her mouth. "Rich, full-bodied flavor. Hot, steamy and perfect to wake up to in the morning. Yeah, you're like coffee. A thousand times better, but like that." Dipping his head, he feathered his lips across hers. "I'm thinking it's time I gave some of the thousand back."

Maya let him boost her onto the counter, draped her arms around his neck. "You've got only an hour, Lieutenant. Better start counting."

TAL'S HEAD WAS A WAR ZONE. His heart? Gone. His dilemma? Of the two he faced, his feelings for Maya won by a landslide. Everything and everyone else could crash and burn.

Drake should have been at the station but wasn't. Perine had managed to slip under the radar again. No surprise there. Nate wasn't answering his phone, and after a loud argument with Captain Sellers, who was grumpily filling in for Drake, Tal found himself saddled with McGraw, who happened to be nursing the granddaddy of hangovers.

"Anything louder than a whisper, and I'll shoot you where you sit," the fraud cop croaked as he climbed into the Mustang. Mouth open, he let his head topple back onto the leather headrest. "I feel motion. Did I make it to your car?"

"Unfortunately." Tal glanced at the cockeyed cup of coffee in McGraw's hand. "Spill that, Gene, and I'll shoot you where you sit."

McGraw rested the cup on his thigh.

"Where'd you go after the hospital last night?" Tal asked him.

"The Tank. Piece of crap cop bar, if you ask me." McGraw took a sip of coffee and made a face. "My leg hurt like a bitch after that loony in the chair broadsided me. I should have arrested him for operating a motorized vehicle under the influence. What about you? Did you get lucky or just wet?"

"None of your business, Detective."

"Answer noted and filed. Where's the doc?"

"At the hospital, under heavy guard."

"Perine?"

"That's the sixty-four-thousand-dollar question."

McGraw gulped another mouthful, then winced. "That was some cozy party in the Deco Room last night. Did Drake explain his presence?"

"I gather the request came from the chief's office."

"Three'll get you ten he was wearing his new watch."

The radio cut in with a loud crackle. McGraw groped for it. "What?"

"Message for Lieutenant Talbot." The dispatcher matched his snappish tone. "Snitch named Hopper says he's got something for you, Tal. Wants you to meet him at Merta's at twenty-three hundred hours."

Tal picked up McGraw's wrist. His watch read nineteen-thirty. "Why the lag?"

"He didn't say. Called it a big bulletin. Said it would be worth your while to show. The way he garbled it out, I was hard-pressed to understand that much. What's he on, anyway?"

"I've never thought to ask. Take McGraw and me off the board until midnight."

"Do I get a reason, in case the captain asks?"

"Yeah." Letting Perine's face slide through his head, Tal swung the Mustang into a U-turn. "Tell him we're going after a big fish."

IT WAS ANOTHER CRAZY NIGHT. Three heart attacks, a fatal stroke, two aneurysms, three severed appendages on two separate people and six big-time overdoses. And those were just the highlights.

The longest break Maya got all double shift was fifteen minutes. Jamie was barking at everyone, including the patients, Cassie Styles had turned into a major klutz and Maya's police guards—an absurd half dozen of them tonight—were interrogating everyone in sight.

Enough, she decided when one of them started grilling a teen with a nose ring and symptoms of blood poisoning. Pulling out her cell, she punched in Tal's number.

"What is it, Maya?"

"Tell your watchdogs to back off or go home. I've got an incensed father who's threatening a lawsuit against our hospital and your department. He claims two of your officers bullied his eighteen-year-old son."

"Would this angry father be a lawyer?"

"Beside the point, Lieutenant."

"Give him my number, and we'll talk tomorrow. Right now I'm busy."

In the background she heard loud music and even louder voices. "I didn't know you were a punk rock fan."

"What I am is working my way through a dive filled with addicts, sharks and hookers, all of whom are smoking cigarettes, less than half of which contain tobacco. And I'm here with a hungover McGraw, breathing secondhand smoke and seriously rethinking my choice of careers."

"So, not a punk rock fan then."

"I'm meeting an informant. With luck, he'll have some news on Falcon."

The lounge door swung open, and Jamie motioned her to hurry up. "Gotta go, Tal. My crushed foot's arrived. Breathe as little as possible, and be careful."

"Back at you, Doc."

She wanted to add more, but Cassie rushed in. "There's a woman in treatment room three with an arrow in her side."

"An arrow?" Tal repeated.

"The things you see when you don't have a camera."

His response, if he made one, was lost in Jamie's distantly sarcastic, "Patient's bleeding all over the gurney, Doctor."

Maya dropped her cell in the pocket of her lab coat and followed Cassie at a run.

A trip through hell had nothing on this night.

"How'd you know about the time rewind?" McGraw demanded. He puffed a little as they jogged through the trash-strewn alley behind the bar. "Snitch says twenty-three hundred at Merta's, but you meet him ninety minutes early at some underground rat hole that's gone through five name changes in the past six months."

"Hopper's been walking the fence for two decades, Gene. He gets a kick out of using clever codes."

"Used to rat for Drake, didn't he?"

"And Nate." Tal cast him a level look. "And you."

"Which is how I know he's a thirty percenter at best. You pay him the twenty and what do you get? Squat."

"You pay Hopper twenty, you're lucky to be at thirty percent. Nate gave him double that amount back when he was pounding the pavement."

"What do you figure made Tyler's chirp relocate to the Ricolini Brothers warehouse?"

"Last place his boss would look, I imagine."

McGraw glanced behind them, into the dark. "Why do I feel like we're being tailed?"

"Because you're paranoid?"

"Or maybe because Perine owns that hole we just left."

"He did. He sold the place two months ago."

"To one of his own dummy corporations." McGraw snapped his fingers. "Put your brain in drive, Lieutenant. He's done the same thing a dozen times over the past two years."

They'd reached the car. Tal unlocked it and made a quick area sweep.

He'd felt the tail McGraw had mentioned earlier, but he didn't sense it now. Good or bad? he wondered and, for a moment, let his instincts prevail.

"You have to actually get in and turn the key before we can leave, Talbot."

McGraw's mocking tone brought a ghost of a smile

to Tal's face. Then his eyes landed on a split trash bag in the alley. The damaged side spewed fast-food containers and broken plastic and sent a sudden visual snapshot to the forefront of his brain.

He'd seen something last night. Something he'd managed to dismiss, even though, dammit, he'd recognized it and should have acknowledged it.

As it tended to, one visual reminder spurred an even more disturbing memory. Swearing, Tal yanked the door open and got in.

"What?" A baffled McGraw looked around before he followed. "Did you see something?"

"Thought it." Tal popped the siren out and on. "Hopper's been around for a lot of years."

"And what? You think he's going senile?"

"I think he's screwing us."

"With false information?"

Squealing out from the alley to the street, Tal indicated the radio. "Request uniform backup at the Ricolini Brothers warehouse. Our ETA's fifteen minutes."

"If we fly, maybe. Otherwise—"

"Do it, McGraw." He swerved the Mustang around a garbage truck and shot through a red light.

The detective held on but made the call. "Do I get a clue, or do we play twenty questions?"

"We lost our tail after we talked to Hopper. I'm betting we're not the only ones he sold his information to."

"But how could Perine— Hell!" McGraw thumped the glove box. "He got someone in the department, someone who's on his payroll, to make contact with your rat fink informant. Cop tail follows us, has his own chat with Hopper, makes the call that sends one of Perine's lackeys to the warehouse. Hopper puts two ticks on the scorecard and walks away, whistling, while he counts his cash." The detective ground his teeth. "I'm gonna off that little mother."

"Do that, but call Nate first."

"And say what?"

The back end of the Mustang swung out as Tal took the next turn. "Tell him we're en route to a fish fry at Perine's old waterfront haunt. Then try and locate Drake."

FALCON HUDDLED, shivered, ate cold beans spooned up with rye bread and listened to the moan of a slow-moving cargo ship.

Sweat dribbled down his spine. Was he safe here? He didn't feel safe. Didn't feel anything but terrified.

He'd done what he could, short of going for official sanctuary. How could he do that when he didn't know which cops to trust? There were rotten apples at every level. Talbot might be straight, but then again, he might not.

Don't move, he reminded himself. Don't make a sound. Wait for the light. Easier to see when the sun comes up.

If the sun came up. It hadn't for Adam Tyler.

Dropping his head to his knees, Falcon gave it several painful thumps. He'd been stupid to walk away from Perine. More stupid to hook up with a cop.

The sound of a side door opening below stopped the thumping and brought his head up. Slowly. Breath held, hands balled, knuckles bone-white.

The silence stretched out, turned the dribble of sweat into a river.

Then the footsteps started.

Chapter Fifteen

"Evening, Dr. S."

In her office for a computer update, Maya raised her head. "McVey?" Suspicion crept in as her eyes traveled to the wall clock. "It's after midnight. Why are you here?" Concern overcame doubt. "Does your hand hurt?"

He wiggled grime-encrusted fingers above a badly soiled bandage. "All the parts work, but it still burns a little."

Shoving suspicion aside, Maya blanked her monitor. "I've got a few minutes before I have to go upstairs. Do you want me to take a look?"

"Please."

Irritated by the lingering tremor in her stomach, she motioned him toward the door. "Treatment room four. You picked a good time to show. It was wild earlier, but not so much now."

"Bad wind blows people in, huh?" When he smiled, he resembled a wolf, fangs bared, cheeks hollow.

Okay, now she was noticing too much. She'd never felt threatened by him before, and she wouldn't start tonight. Besides, there were guards everywhere. She spied two of them as she preceded McVey along the corridor.

"I came in earlier," he told her. "But you were busy, so you probably didn't see me. Is Witch—uh, Nurse Hazell working tonight?"

"You're a lucky man, McVey. She went off-shift an hour ago." Maya pushed through the treatment-room door. A pair of guards detached themselves from the shadows to stand outside.

McVey backed up onto the table. "Why so many cops?"

"Ask Lieutenant Talbot." Out of habit, Maya drew the folding screen across. Then she unwrapped his hand. "Oh, double yuck, McVey. There's gum on your bandage."

He lowered his head. "Could be I went through a trash can or two."

"Looking for cigarette butts?"

"Finding's cheaper than buying."

"It's also grosser."

The grin sucked his cheeks in even more and gave his face a cadaverous cast. "You're pretty when you're grossed out. Was your mother pretty, too?"

"Very." Maya pressed a thumb to his palm, watched it go from dirty white to dirty red. "You do know what water's for?"

"Heard stories. How long's she been gone?"

"Seven years." Only Maya's eyes came up. "Why the interest?"

"Making conversation, is all." He shifted on the table. "Are you and the lieutenant together now?"

"If I answer that, do I get to ask a personal question?"

"Maybe."

She smiled, watched his face. "Afraid I'll discover some dirty little secret, McVey?"

"No." But he dropped his gaze and made her heart beat just a little faster.

Maya heard voices outside, then saw an out-of-breath Cassie scurry around the screen. "Dr. Santino, there's something happening down in the cafeteria. Guys on drugs with guns. I think one of them got the cashier." She gestured rapidly in the general direction. "Dr. Driscoll's not here. Nurse Hazell says you should come."

Maya's system jittered, then steadied. "Stay here," she told McVey. "Don't leave, and don't follow."

She heard distant gunshots, three of them. Beside her, Cassie's eyes went huge.

"Are you okay?" Maya set calming hands on the nurse's shoulders.

"I think so. Scared. But this is what it's all about, right?"

"Baptism by fire. We get through it. McVey?" She turned back. Exasperation flooded in when she spied the flask he was attempting to cap and tuck away. "If you tell me you're carrying that for medicinal purposes, I'm going to hand you over to Nurse Hazell. Give." She extended her hand, palm up.

He hesitated but reached inside his jacket. Maya glimpsed the dirty red lining, heard another shot and changed her hand position to a stop sign. "I have to go. Just don't drink any more—" She broke off when an unexpected image formed. Her eyes returned briefly to his jacket.

The fuzzy memory floated in her head, of something she'd seen last night. Something not quite right. Something…

"Doctor?" Cassie's voice quivered. "We really need to go."

"I know. I just… I know."

She shoved the foggy memory into the back of her mind. The current crisis took precedence.

"Don't drink," she said to McVey.

"Which entrance…?" Cassie began, then widened her eyes and finished with a squeaky "Doctor?"

Maya heard another shot in the distance. But it was the closer sound that captured her attention and, for some reason, sent a chill skating along her spine.

It wasn't much. A tiny swish. A drift of air stirring her hair from behind.

The thud was louder, an unmistakable sound. She knew it was McVey's body hitting the floor, even before Cassie clutched at her arm. Containing her reaction, Maya braced for the worst.

She didn't want to look, was terrified to see what some part of her brain already recognized as horrible, monstrous truth.

He was here, in this room, less than three feet away, waiting for her to turn.

Waiting to kill her as he'd killed Adam.

TAL SMELLED BLOOD IN THE damp warehouse air. It mingled with other odors—green fruit, day-old fish, machine oil and wooden crates as ancient as the hull of a beached boat he'd explored as a kid.

"We were making our rounds and saw someone running out." A warehouse security guard twice as broad as McGraw crouched next to Tal. "Took us thirty minutes to find the body. Not like last time, when the guy was lying in the middle of the floor. This one had a camp stove, food and blankets. Must've been hiding out here for a few days."

Tal tucked his gun into his waistband, took in the half-eaten loaf of rye bread, the cooler with its melting block of ice, the empty bottle of scotch.

Uniforms could handle the details here. Falcon was dead, shot in the back of his neck. One bullet, fired from the open stairway. Orlando Perine's trademark send-off, or so the story went.

It also went that the man hadn't squeezed his own triggers for years. But then, Tal reflected, he hadn't heard everything, had he? He hadn't been part of the ongoing investigation. He didn't know what Nate and his captain knew, what they'd seen, what one or both of them might have missed.

He tried Nate's number as he stood. No answer. He punched in Drake's home phone and his cell. Nothing. With a last look at Falcon's dying expression—bug-eyed and horrified—he left a uniformed sergeant in charge and headed for the stairs.

McGraw strode over as Tal stepped off the last tread. "There's no sign of forced entry. Killer knew how to get in. It's like Tyler's death, only not so open."

"We've beefed up security since that officer was murdered," a second warehouse guard revealed. "The Ricolinis, they don't want any more trouble. With anyone."

Tal speed-dialed Maya's cell. He got her voice mail, swore, left a brief message. Then he called Dole.

"Where is she?" he demanded when the officer picked up.

"Treating a patient," was the crackling reply. "It's been a zoo here tonight, Lieutenant, but she's safe in treatment room four with that homeless guy and a young nurse."

"McVey?"

"Say again, Tal? Sorry, I'm on the edge of a dead zone. We're having…" His voice petered out, came back. "Think she's safe enough. I've got the exits covered…."

This time the line went dead. As it did, Tal spotted a

twitch of movement, largely masked by a series of tightly packed shelves. Flipping his phone closed, he yanked the gun from his jeans, made a head motion. "McGraw."

"What is it?"

"Lurch. Behind the rum."

"The lug from the Marbel Club?" An evil grin split the detective's face. "Isn't that nice. Puppet wants to pay his last respects."

Tal scoped the area, top to bottom, side to side. "Can you create a diversion?" he asked the warehouse guard.

"I'll do my best." Separating himself, the man whistled upward. "Hey! Got ourselves a scumbag thief at the north entrance." He took off in that direction, away from the rum. "With me," he shouted to his co-workers. "Fan out. Surround the entry doors."

Footsteps thundered in the cavernous warehouse. A crate hit the ground. Tal split from McGraw and watched for movement between the shadowed shelves.

He didn't expect Perine's man to be fooled, only momentarily distracted.

As another crate splintered, the shadows shifted.

McGraw's voice reached him. "Got a runner, Talbot."

Tal took off. If they circled in opposite directions, they could intercept the guy.

The rows ran straight, with a minimum number of breaks. Most of the openings that did exist were blocked with machinery. Tal vaulted over a line of barrels, heard footfalls pounding on the concrete floor. A light flared, shone in his eyes.

He ducked sideways, felt his adrenaline pump. Oh, yeah, this was good. Going in for the kill—in a figurative but still enormously satisfying sense.

In front of him, a shape materialized. The light

bobbed, searching but not finding anything this time. Tal stayed low, ran without making a sound.

Unable to expose anyone, the man behind the light doused it and took off again. He wasn't fast enough. Tal tackled him from behind. Together, they flew over a steel container and landed hard against the end of a shelf.

McGraw called out, "Got one over here, Lieutenant. My ninety-year-old granny moves faster than this lumbering ox."

So there were two. Ignoring the jangle in his head, Tal flipped his man over. A black knitted cap gave way to features grimly set and taut with the strain of capture.

Eyes glittering, Tal shoved his gun under the man's chin. "Looks like you have some explaining to do, Mr. Perine."

"He's got a gun, Dr. Santino."

With a glance at Cassie's terrified face, Maya steeled herself and turned. She couldn't do anything at first, other than stare at the gun barrel.

Later, the scene might make some kind of horrible, twisted sense, but for now, it was all fear. For her life, for Cassie's and, oh God, McVey's.

"Don't move, Dr. Santino." The man in front of her wagged his gun as if it were a finger. "He isn't dead. I'm not completely devoid of emotion. I'm just a really pissed-off cop who's sick of watching fat cats like Perine do their dirty deeds, dust off, flip us the bird, then go right back to their business pursuits—those being to cheat, steal, launder and, when the occasion warrants, kill." A reptilian grin appeared. "You getting the picture?"

Cassie's fingernails bit into Maya's arm. The pain

helped her focus. She still had to swallow around the ball of fear that had climbed into her throat.

"There's no way out of here, except past the guards Tal posted," she told him. Not true, since he'd obviously gotten past them to get in, but that was terror for you, combined with the certain knowledge that she needed to keep him talking.

His grin widened. "Spoken without a tremor. But dead wrong, unfortunately… Oh, no, sorry." He winked. "That's for later. For now—" he made an exaggerated motion toward the door that connected treatment rooms four and three "—we'll exit this way. Sorry you have to come along for the ride, Nurse…." He squinted at her badge. "Styles. I've never been big on excess baggage, but needs dictate action in these circumstances."

"Needs?" Maya asked.

The man nodded. "Needs, wants, just rewards. Call it what you will. I deserve more, and I'm going to have or, more correctly, keep having it. Finally, finally, this stalled-out mess is moving forward. I got Falcon tonight, shot him dead, very close to the place where I shot Adam. But I have to tell you it's been a nightmare of a journey.

"First, I had to wait for him to surface. He did, of course, more than once, but give the traitorous rat his due. Somehow he always managed to outmaneuver me. And being a thorough and incisive sort of man, I'm not easily outmaneuvered." The grin vanished. "Now, move, the pair of you, through the door. Doctor first, then nurse. Slightest sound, the nurse dies. Got that, Doc?"

Maya regulated her breathing. She could handle this, think through it, past it. The man was a murderer. Don't agitate. Stall.

When Cassie's feet remained glued, their captor made an impatient sound and reached for her. But then he stopped and smiled. "Let's do this another way, shall we?" And he grabbed Maya's arm instead.

He was stronger and better trained than Falcon. He had her arm locked painfully behind her before Cassie reacted with a gasp.

"Go, Nurse Styles. Not a peep," he growled as he jammed his gun into the side of Maya's neck. "Either of you."

"Where?" Cassie managed to ask.

"Side door, side door, staff door, service elevator. Anything happens, bang, you're dead."

"And you're caught," Maya pointed out softly.

"You think?" He set his mouth close to her ear. "Or is it possible that, like Orlando Perine, I have a cop or two on my payroll? Is it also possible perhaps that the ones I don't pay have been dispatched to another area of the hospital? Like, say, the cafeteria? Junkies on a drug-induced shooting spree. Would that be coincidence or a clever ploy? I'll let you decide. While you do as I say!"

The harsh command got Cassie moving. Across the threshold, into the adjoining treatment room. Empty, Maya noted, and undoubtedly secured from the inside. He wouldn't overlook a detail like that.

The medicine room came next. Cassie walked like a malfunctioning robot, with her head perpetually half-swiveled and her limbs almost too awkward to control.

Maya's left arm ached. Any more upward force, and he'd dislocate her shoulder. But then, experience would have taught him just how much pressure could be applied.

"Finally, we arrive." At the elevator he held Maya close, kept the gun pressed to her neck. "Push the button, Nurse Styles. Then step aside. No, not up. Down. Morgue level. It's quiet at night in the hospital nether regions. Before I rose to captain, I spent many a year prowling the bowels of many a hospital." He pushed them into the elevator as he spoke, then rubbed Maya's hair with his cheek. "Soft," he murmured. "No wonder Tal's so smitten. Shall we talk, Maya my dear? Stand among the dead and discuss your ex-husband's last words?"

The elevator ground to a halt. Cassie's eyes were huge in her chalk-white face. "Exit stage right," he told her, then clucked his tongue in her wake. "Don't know if she's up to the E.R., Doctor. Day surgery might be more suitable." The false humor vanished, and he wrenched a little harder on her arm. "What did Adam say, Maya? What did your oh-so-clever but, unfortunately, not-clever-enough ex-husband tell you before he died? I want his exact words."

She gritted her teeth against the pain. "I gave my statement."

"Oh, well, I'll just trot downtown and reread it, shall I?" He gave a hard shake. "I know what it says. What I don't know is what it means. 'Big fish, small pond.' Explain."

Maya scrambled through her thoughts. "He wasn't specific. Everything I know is in my statement."

"You understood Adam, knew how his mind worked."

Razor-thin blades sliced along her arm and into the vertebrae of her neck. "No one knew how Adam's mind worked."

"He told you not to trust anyone. Think hard and fast, Doctor. Your nurse might do something stupid, and I'm a better shot than I ever let on. In the back's my— Oh, no, sorry again. It's Perine's specialty. What I am is an excellent mimic. Next to impossible to tell my handiwork from that of the genuine article. Now, did Adam mention any names in the don't-trust column?"

Maya's head swam. She fought to clear it. "No, no names."

"None at all, at any time?"

"No." Could she knee him? Probably not. Knock the gun from his hand? Not before he shot her. Or Cassie.

With a sigh, he removed the gun from her neck and pointed it at the terrified nurse, whose mouth was rounded into a frozen O. "Give me something, or the redhead dies."

Maya made another fast scramble, although it was difficult with a cry of pain clamoring to escape and her vision beginning to waver. "He said…" She hissed when he jerked her arm. "He said it would be a major mistake."

"What would?"

"Ah…" Another fiery spike of pain sheared through her. "To trust any crooked fish who'd want to spend his life in a small pond, I suppose."

To her astonishment, he let the gun drop just a fraction—while he chuckled?

Insane, Maya realized hazily. Not merely cold and borderline sociopathic, but clinically crazy.

"You make my point in spades, Doctor." The chortle died as he inclined his head to hiss in her ear. "Cops are small fish compared to the Perines of the world. Small fish, living, working and sometimes losing themselves in a small, small pond. Perine, on the other hand, he's your big shark who left the ocean to make the pond we call Miami his own. And give the man credit, he knows how to work his territorial waters to maximum advantage. But then again, after much observation, frustration and self-reevaluation, so do I." The gun snapped back, this time jabbing the underside of her chin. "What else, Doctor?"

"He wanted me to handle his affairs, his will, make sure his sister and brother received what he'd intended for them to have."

"Sister and brother," he repeated. "Nothing for you?"

"The condo, but we went through it."

His lips moving against her hair brought a shudder of revulsion—and a deep chuckle. "You don't like that, do you? You don't want me to do it again. Give me something that leads to the information, and I'll stop."

"You mean you'll shoot me," Maya said flatly.

"Quick and painless," he promised. "Otherwise... Well, let's say a police officer learns a great deal about the merits of slow torture over the years. More, Maya." He kissed her temple, straight-armed his gun. "You've got three seconds before Nurse Styles precedes you on the short but unpleasant journey from corridor to slab. Three, two, one..."

Chapter Sixteen

Tal shoved past a paramedic at the emergency entrance. He was tempted to gut-punch Maya's primary guard, but he settled for hauling him aside.

"How the hell could six of you lose her?"

"There was a problem." Dole dragged a hand through his hair. "Tal, I swear to God, I had no choice. Two guys blew into the cafeteria, whipped out guns and started shooting the place up. No one got killed, but Sellers pulled three of us off guard duty to help security deal with the situation. Even so, we had the exits from the treatment room covered."

"Even so," McGraw said as he holstered his gun, "one of you screwed up. Or was bought off."

Dole's mouth compressed. "It wasn't me, Detective."

"No." Tal forced a calm he was far from feeling, ran his gaze around the waiting area. "I'm guessing Oldman."

"Get real," McGraw scoffed. "Oldie's a twenty-year man with a hot second wife."

"Who likes diamonds, designer clothes and power-shopping trips to New York three times a year." Tal pulled Dole with him down the hall. "Where was he positioned? Exactly."

The officer pointed. "Service corridor. Not much traffic."

"Show me."

Dole obeyed, via a conduit of interconnecting hallways.

"Where is he now?" Tal asked while McGraw inspected the surrounding area.

"Searching for Dr. Santino." Dole sighed. "Or so I thought. I'm sorry, Tal. I was in charge. It didn't occur to me to question Drake's choices."

"Why would it?" Leaving the safety off, Tal retucked his weapon. His gaze shifted to the top of the service elevator. "Which way?" he wondered aloud.

He pressed both call buttons. The elevator nearest to the med room ascended. The one farthest away came down.

"Morgue and subbasement are below us, right?"

Dole nodded. "Both creep shows. You want the sub?"

"Morgue. You're sure he came this far?"

"If he took her, he could only have gotten out through that door. I stationed myself between treatment rooms three and four, put Carstairs on the med room and Oldman on the corridor. And if you tell me I can't trust my own partner, I'm quitting right now."

"You'll get your pension." Tal raised his voice. "I'm going down to the morgue, McGraw. Find Oldman."

Tal punched the morgue-level button, refused to visualize the worst. Maya wouldn't die. He wouldn't let it happen. She'd been the last person to talk to Adam. She knew that, and she was smart enough to use it.

"Lieutenant." Dole snagged his jacket sleeve when the elevator dinged. "Remember we don't know where Oldman went."

But Tal already had his gun drawn.

The doors opened with a low hum. Unfortunately, a hum read like a roar in an echo chamber.

The elevator continued its descent. When it clanked to a halt, Tal let the silence wash over him. He waited, motionless, until he picked up a murmur of sound to his right. With a quick shoulder check, he started toward it. No sound, no wasted motion, no idea what he'd be facing when he located them.

It wasn't Perine. It never had been, or not for several years. The great pretender, Tal thought. Best he'd ever encountered. Best and most deadly.

He heard a man now, and a woman. Maya.

Relief so strong it momentarily blurred his vision spiked through grim purpose. Unfortunately, the thunder of silence made the words they spoke incomprehensible.

Tal worked his way closer, thought he heard the elevator again. It was probably Dole, returning from the subbasement. Two guns would be better than one, but only if Maya was clear. If not, he'd be forced to try reason. Or trickery.

How did you trick an illusionist, a man who'd been fooling everyone around him for…Tal had no idea how long. At the Ricolini Brothers warehouse, Perine had measured the time in years. Two had been his estimate, though longer was certainly possible.

Perine said he'd known someone was emulating his style. He'd known it was a cop. He'd even known the man's name. What he hadn't known was how to stop him without screwing himself up. Catch-22—or so it seemed, until his ex-employee Falcon had contacted him and begged for access to the charity party. Failure there had led to a warehouse meeting tonight. Unfortunately, Falcon had been dead when Orlando and his man arrived.

Ahead of Tal, the corridor teed off, faded to black in both directions. The voices came from a point several yards and more than one turn away. Where the hell was Oldman? he wondered. Down here, playing lookout, or upstairs, playing dumb?

He glanced into the darkness on both sides as he continued moving. He couldn't hear Maya now. Why?

Picking up the pace, he threw everything forward, all his senses. A mistake for any cop—one he paid for when he glimpsed a movement in his peripheral vision.

And spied the gun that emerged from the shadows.

"Dr. Santino...?"

Cassie's watery plea had Maya using her free hand to tug on her captor's forearm. "Don't shoot her. I'm thinking. I am. He, Adam told me his brother was a crash addict, he didn't want him to have his car."

"And?"

Cassie's voice cracked. "He—he gave you two sets of keys."

"One set was for his condo, the other was for the car." Maya sucked back a sharp breath when her arm was jerked upward again. Frustration joined fear. "There was an extra key on Tal's ring. It unlocked a safe in Adam's condo. But there was nothing inside." She swallowed a gasp as lightning zaps of pain made her vision wobble again.

He made a snorting sound. "In the business, we call that a decoy, Doctor. Red herring, prop, false trail." But he stopped, relaxed his grip somewhat and appeared to consider it. "A decoy. Hmm. And Tal got the car?"

"The lieutenant insisted," Cassie put in, with a tremor. "I was there. I heard."

"Well, well." He set his mouth against Maya's temple, returned the gun to her neck. "Something there, you think?"

"You know the car was searched," she said. "At least three times. Once by McGraw."

He sneered. "McGraw wouldn't spot a clue if it crawled up and bit his ass, screaming. Go through the list again. Did Adam fish? Was there gear in the trunk? A tackle box? Something rolled up in one of the lures?"

Maya shook her head. "He didn't fish. There was a jacket, an old, battered one."

"Lined?"

"The lining was torn. There was nothing hidden inside it."

"What else?"

"Movies, music. Downloads mostly." She hesitated, but only for a moment. Had the shadow to her left just stirred? "Eight-tracks," she added quickly. "Two of them. Abba."

"No player?"

"Not anymore, and never in the car."

"Where are the tapes?" His lips thinned. "Where, Maya? Or it's good night, ladies."

"They're in the glove box. Adam's brother wants them."

"Does he now?" She heard it in his voice, the satisfaction of a hard-won victory. "Well, that is an intriguing piece of news." His tone took on a velvet edge. "I believe we may be on track—no pun intended."

With an abrupt and unexpected motion, he released her trapped arm, whipped a second gun out from underneath his jacket and pointed it into the darkness to his left. "One more step, Lieutenant, and the doc's dead. Make a grab for my hand, Maya, and I blow your lover away."

Maya stopped her aching arm from moving. Her eyes fastened on the shadow.

Tal stepped out, hands in sight, his finger clearly off the trigger.

"Let them go." His gaze didn't waver from the older man's face. "I'll do what you want. I'll take you to the car, wherever. Just let Maya and Nurse Styles go back upstairs."

"Live and let die. That the deal, Mr. Bond? Forgive me if I don't trust you, but I did help train you, remember? And now you get to guess. Which of these two triggers is old Nate gonna squeeze first?"

MAYA DIDN'T MOVE. Didn't dare. She simply kept her eyes on Tal's face and prayed he could get through to the man holding her.

Tal came farther into the light, still holding his gun in what looked like a nonthreatening way.

"Come on, Nate," he said evenly. "You don't need to shoot anyone. You can lock us in and leave, grab the eight-tracks and be at the airport before we get out."

The grin in Nate's voice brought a chill, like bony fingers feathering along Maya's spine. "You're not surprised, are you? You've known about me for some time now."

"Suspected," Tal said. "Didn't want to believe. Did everything in my power not to, but the final visual slap put an end to it."

Nate shoved the barrel of the gun a little harder into Maya's neck. "Move and you're dead, Doc. Ditto, Nurse Styles, although I'm not sure you could budge if your life depended on it. Again, no pun intended." His tone roughened. "How, Tal?"

Tal's gaze stayed on his old friend's face. "Milk in your fridge was weeks past its sell-by date. Newest magazine in the stack was six months old. You don't live in that house, Nate. You just drop in from time to time. We got lucky finding you there that night, or you got lucky being there. I saw the timers on the lamps. Lights are preset to go out at one in the morning and set to come on whenever. Tall hedges between you and the neighboring houses. A park across the street. No one to see or wonder."

"It's a piss-poor neighborhood. Lower Slobovia. Most of the people wouldn't care if Jack the Ripper moved in as long as he kept his distance."

"That makes it easier. Neighbors on both sides rent. Renters don't pay attention to the people around them. They come. They go. Perfect setup."

"And so, suspicion sets in. Next clue?"

"You wanted me to think Drake was dirty."

"Well, hell, I made him look it, didn't I? Gave him a truck, rigged that whole I-won-it-in-a-contest deal, at no small expense to myself. Doubts raised, answers provided, but the niggle remained. You were looking his way. What else?"

"The tap on my phone. Even Perine couldn't have pulled that one off. But we played poker right before Maya and I drove up to see Miadora. You heard me talking to her neighbor, to her, to Maya. Knowing about the trip made it easy for you. You didn't have Falcon, but you could send a couple of your people ahead. Their assignment? Run us off the road, grab Maya. Maybe you'd score the information, and to hell with Adam's snitch. Unfortunately, things didn't go as planned. Your guys screwed up, and an old man died. Count's at four murders, Nate."

"Count's gonna rise, I'm afraid." The barrel of Nate's gun pressed into Maya's carotid artery. "Does Drake know you're here?"

"What do you think?"

"That I might have to kill your captain as well. And him, with that dream truck sitting in his garage, waiting to be let loose just as soon as he can shake this monkey of a case off his back."

"What about the watch, Nate? Your idea or his?"

"Now that's a damn good question, Lieutenant. But then you're a damn good cop. I don't know where that watch came from. I only know it played right into my hands."

"And the vacation?"

"There's a vacation? Huh. Maybe I gave Drake more credit for being straight than he deserves. Possible he's one of Perine's rubber cops, after all. I promise you, he isn't one of mine. Though, as I'm sure you're aware, I do have a few who've kept me as appraised as they can."

"Oldman?"

"Guy has an expensive wife. There's also Harper, Saunders, Cavelli, Moran. Oh, and J. J. Jones. Can't forget him. He's got twenty-five years in fraud. Man's been a font. Speaking of fraud and fonts, did you know that Adam's Falcon, an investment broker by trade, used to work for Perine? His real name's Peter Swindell. Great name for an investment broker, don't you think? Came to work for me two years ago. Don't know why, but I trusted him. My mistake. Not sure what, but something about my methods must have spooked him. Maybe it was those two murders you mentioned. Anyway, I got wind someone had turned.

"A few days later, one of my police sources got wind

of Tyler's score. Two and two make four no matter what side you're on. So I kept my eye on Adam, and, bingo, I got lucky. Shortly after the information was passed to him, he met his contact at the warehouse. Then I got unlucky. Yeah, I offed Tyler, but I missed Falcon. Still, the doc here saw him, so no problem. All I had to do was find him, right? That was easier said than done, let me tell you. However, as I've always maintained, persistence pays. Did in this case. And now here we all are. One last hurdle to clear, and I'm away, with Perine left holding the proverbial bag. Not sure he'll be able to weasel out this time, but we'll see. It won't matter to me in any case."

"That's some plan, Nate," Tal remarked.

"I'll take that as a compliment, Lieutenant."

Maya fought back a shiver when he shoved his gun in deeper.

"I do believe you're moving, my dear," Nate observed coldly. "Could it be you want to distract me, give your lover a chance to shoot? He's a marksman, you know. He could do it. But then you'd be dead, and the shock of that might slow him down a tad." He raised his voice. "What do you think, McGraw? Which of the two of you would hit his mark first? Step out of the shadows if you please. Same hands-up position as the lieutenant here."

"And if I don't?" McGraw challenged from the dark.

Maya felt Nate shrug. "Then my guess is Tal will turn and shoot you. Because his pretty doc will be as dead as me, and that'll only leave Nurse Styles standing. Into the light, or there'll be a lot more corpses down here than today's tally sheets can account for."

"Do it, Gene," Tal told the detective.

Three seconds passed like three hours to Maya while a stubborn McGraw dragged his feet. "I caught Oldman upstairs. Your rat was trying to scuttle out the back door."

The chuckle in Maya's ear had every square inch of her skin crawling. "He did his job. I don't care what happens to him, or to any of them. Contingency plan in effect, boys. I'm off to parts unknown. Would have preferred to milk the system awhile longer, but all good things must end sometime, right? Really, if I were you, Gene, I'd lose the gun. Because even if Tal doesn't turn on you when his lady's gone, you'll be a dead man. You're not half the shot I am, and I have a shield."

"Load of crap," muttered McGraw. He held fast until Tal reached out his free hand and snatched the gun away.

"Are you mad?" The fraud cop strode out. "He couldn't have taken both of us down."

"Maybe not." For the first time since he'd appeared, Tal allowed his gaze to leave Nate's face and settle on Cassie Styles. "But she could have."

IT HAPPENED IN AN INSTANT. Sound, motion, at least two guns going off.

Maya glimpsed some of it, but in a freakish, off-kilter way that made her feel like she'd been dropped into a Batman rerun.

She fell, or was flung, into Cassie, whose head hit the wall with a dull thwack. McGraw shouted. Another shot exploded. The corridor went black.

Maya's head spun. Blood trickled down her cheek. Had she been grazed by a bullet or had she fallen into the wall with Cassie?

"What the hell happened to the lights?" McGraw bellowed. Then something thumped, and he went silent.

Maya scrambled to her knees. She heard Cassie moan next to her and checked for a pulse. Weak but steady.

The sound of a fight in progress had her searching her pockets for her penlight. She clicked it on. "Tal?"

Labored breathing reached her. Was it Nate? Was he running? Where was Tal?

A persistent throbbing in her temple made the black spots behind her eyes do a gleeful jig. She was climbing to her feet when a pair of hands caught her waist and hauled her the rest of the way up.

"It's me," Tal said in her ear. "I knocked Nate into a door. He knocked me off balance and disappeared. Take the nurse and get out of here."

"But she's—"

"Working for Nate? No, she isn't. I just wanted to throw him off. Go. I can handle him."

"If you can find him."

"He'll find me."

Together, they pulled a groggy Cassie upright.

"Where's McGraw?" Maya asked.

"Nate winged him with his backup. He'll be fine. You and the nurse get out. Take the stairs."

"But—"

"Do it, Maya." He kissed her hard on the mouth. "For me."

She saw his gun in silhouette, felt her heart rate accelerate. But she did as he asked and dragged the groggy nurse toward the stairwell.

Fear for Tal's life thrummed through her. Nate would kill him without a second thought. But he'd have to find him first, and with the lights off—Tal's doing, she suspected—the older man should be at a disadvantage.

"I can't see," Cassie said thickly. "I don't know this area."

Maya did, but in the dark, it was like stumbling through a maze.

Everything had gone eerily silent. There were no more thuds or scrapes, no grunts, nothing except the hum of the AC and their footsteps on the vinyl-tiled floor.

Maya drew a mental map. Where were the fire stairs? Through the door and left, she thought. Then she glanced back. Where was Tal? Equally important, where was Nate?

"Doctor?"

"We're good." She pressed reassuring fingers into Cassie's arm. "Almost there."

"I don't work for him."

"I know. Keep moving."

"It's so dark."

"We need to be quiet, Cassie." She cracked open an interior door, trying to orient herself.

She was pulling out her penlight again when the gunshots erupted behind her.

TAL KNEW Nate's night vision was only fair. Which meant he had to watch out for tricks. With less than three quarters of his attention fixed on finding his old friend, he figured the advantage swung strongly to Nate's side.

He'd sent Maya to safety. He felt certain Nate had doubled back to the service elevators. But what if he'd guessed wrong? He was a good cop, but still human. Nate had outwitted him in the past. Big-time. He'd been dirty and smart enough to frame Perine, who, while unquestionably a criminal, was probably only about half as bad as he appeared.

The corridor stretched out in front of him like a black hole. Tal knew where the light switch was. He'd hit the thing initially. Unfortunately, in blinding Nate, he'd hindered himself and McGraw. And Maya. But it was a chance he'd had to take.

A barely perceptible scrape brought him up short. He adjusted his grip, kept his gun angled skyward.

The scrape became a snap. Then a single light flared, slanted outward from a small utility room.

Even as he swung his gun down, Tal knew he'd walked right into it. You couldn't outmaneuver a crafty veteran on three-quarters brainpower.

The bullet exploded out of Nate's gun, caught Tal in the chest, below his right shoulder. He got off a shot of his own but had no idea if it hit or not. The third crack barely registered.

He hadn't taken a bullet to the head, but he might as well have, because everything inside it went red.

He felt his muscles go numb, saw the floor rise up to meet him.

By the time he landed, the red had turned to black.

THE SHOTS SOUNDED like cannon fire to Maya, but that could be grisly imagination rather than truth. Three bullets had been fired, and she couldn't tell if they'd come from the same gun or not.

"Please let Tal be safe," she prayed.

"Doctor?"

"Keep going, Cassie."

"Those gunshots were close."

So much for imagination. "Door's at the end of this corridor, to the right."

"Are you sure?"

"Yes," Maya lied and pushed again. "Move faster, okay?"

"My head hurts. It's making me dizzy. But I'll try."

Maya was propelling the nurse around a wide jut of wall when the lights came on, icy-white and blinding.

She swore her heart stopped beating.

Nate stood there, less than fifty feet away, at the far end of the corridor. Although rumpled and bruised, he had his gun out and a gleam in his eyes similar to the one she'd seen in Tal's.

"Stand aside, Nurse." When Cassie hesitated, he barked, "Now!"

Maya gave her a firm push, fixed her gaze on Nate's perspiring face.

He swiped a hand over his upper lip. "This was supposed to go down easy, pretty Maya. One dead doctor. Falcon eliminated. Blame falls on Perine."

"Where's Tal?" she asked.

"Dead or dying," he countered, taut-lipped. "I'd have stayed to determine which, but McGraw blundered in with his gun. I knew time was running out. I couldn't allow you to escape. Interruptions and urgency—those two things have become the story of my life. Security showed up at the warehouse in Adam's case. Damn, I had to get out. I took care of Falcon tonight, no problem, but thanks to you and Quick Draw, your lover and my friend might be suffering a slow and painful death as we speak."

Maya's teeth wanted to chatter. "Your friend?" she managed to challenge.

"Was." He swiped his lip again, then blinked to clear his eyes. "Could have gone on being my friend if things had worked out. But then, nothing ever does, and we're left with a mess that will result in me having to exit the country prematurely." Cocking the hammer of his backup weapon, he let a smile steal over his lips. "Bye, Doc. It's been a bittersweet slice."

Maya wasn't entirely sure what happened next. Nate squeezed the trigger; she knew that because she heard the shot. But no bullet sliced through her. Someone had flown out of the shadows, knocked her sideways, then dropped to the floor in a heap.

Before the person landed, she heard another shot, this one from behind.

She saw Nate's eyes widen, watched his jaw go slack. In super-slow motion, his arm fell, and his gun clattered on the tiles.

Shock registered on his face. For a moment, the fingers of his extended hand curled.

"Student outmaneuvers teacher," he choked. And pitched to the floor, face-first.

Maya's shocked eyes zeroed in on the man at her feet. "McVey?" Then she looked behind her and gasped. "Tal! Oh my God…Cassie, take McVey." Pushing to her feet, she ran to Tal.

On his knees, his arms dropping slowly, Tal was breathing hard and bleeding heavily.

"Don't move," Maya ordered. She tore at his T-shirt and gritted her teeth when she saw the bullet wound.

"It's okay," he said in a slurry voice. "Just a scratch."

Then his body went limp, and he toppled into her arms.

Chapter Seventeen

"You removed a bullet from Lieutenant Talbot's chest?" Dressed in pajama pants and flip-flops, Jamie stared at Maya in astonishment. "Driscoll let you do that?"

Exhausted, emotionally and physically, Maya leaned against the hospital wall. "Tal's good. He's in Recovery. Driscoll got here halfway through the surgery. He's running a post-op check, wouldn't let me stay."

"I can't believe you didn't come apart in the O.R."

"Almost did. Am I still standing?"

"Just."

Through a jumble of thoughts—most of them involving Tal—a name snuck in.

"McVey…" She brought her head up. "Where is he?"

Jamie ran her fingers through her badly disordered hair. "Downstairs, I think. I'm not sure, actually. I came straight up. I wanted to explain."

"About you and Perine?"

"I was watching TV. Suddenly, there he was, being led out of a warehouse by police. They said a man inside was dead. I knew you were here, so I phoned, but the duty nurse couldn't find you. Maya, I'm so sorry." Jamie gripped her hands, squeezed. "I should have told you, but I was messed up, confused. I didn't get the volley-ball-coaching gig. Wouldn't have been enough money in it, anyway. But then, a miracle happened. Perine offered me a job as a private nurse for his wife's grand-father. I didn't know what to do. The money part was fantastic, and Renita… Well, you can see my dilemma."

Freeing a hand, Maya touched her friend's cheek. "I understand family problems, Jamie. Look, I'll talk to you nonstop when things settle down, but right now, I need to see McVey. He took a bullet for me, and I don't know why."

"Don't you?"

Maya shook her head at the speculative glint. "He's not my long-lost father. I'd have felt that or known it somehow inside. Yes, he seems familiar, but not that way."

"You don't think."

Maya's gaze traveled to the door, behind which the head of the E.R. was examining the man she loved, the man who'd ultimately saved her life.

She released her breath in a rush. "I don't want to think. I want the truth. Whatever it entails."

"HE'S NOT GOING TO make it, Maya." The attending E.R. physician sighed. "I'm amazed he's held on this long."

Maya looked down at McVey's face. She tried to erase the scruff of beard, flesh out the hollow cheeks. She was so busy doing that, she missed the hand that snaked out to clutch her wrist.

"Dr. Santino…"

His voice was a rasp of barely recognizable sound. She bent over. "I'm here."

"Stay with me?"

She thought of Tal upstairs but squeezed his arm. "You know I will."

His lungs rattled when he spoke. "Like you a lot, Dr. S. It's mostly why I came here." He moved his eyes to look at her. "Not the only reason, though." The fingers attached to her wrist tightened. His voice, already thready, dropped to a whisper. "I was a husband once. Bad husband. Worse father. Need you to do this for me. Tell him I'm sorry. Tell him to be happy. Tell him I wish I could have been the father he deserved. Say goodbye to Tal for me."

HE WAS SWIMMING IN MOLASSES. Thick, black and so heavy, he was tempted to give up and let himself sink.

"He's inside you," his mother raged. "You are what he was. What he is. You are your father...."

For the first time in his life, Tal considered challenging her, but even as the thought occurred to him, the voice he heard changed, softened. Forget a challenge. He wanted to surface.

"The information Falcon gave Adam isn't in either of the eight-tracks," Maya told him from a distance. He felt her kissing his face, touching his hair. "Drake doubts it'll ever be found, or if it is, it'll be pure dumb luck. And speaking of Captain Drake, that new watch you and Nate were wondering about was a twenty-fifth anniversary gift from his wife. She gave him the watch, and he surprised her with a trip to Bali. Two weeks. No kids. Luxury resort with spa. So there you go. Another mystery solved.

"McGraw's fine. He was shot, like you, but only in the arm. He says he's grateful it wasn't you who pulled the trigger. I think he meant that as a compliment. As for Jamie, she got a job offer from Perine. That's what their meeting at the hotel was all about.

She wanted to say no, because, well, she thought he was trying to kill me. But she listened to him, because she needs money to keep her daughter in a program for troubled teens. Now that we know Orlando had nothing to do with this, she's reconsidering his offer. Drake thinks she's insane, but my guess is he's trying to clean up his act.

"There's more I could tell you, but I'll save it for when I'm sure you can hear me, which better be soon, because I love you, Tal, and I want to say that to your face."

His lips curved. Somewhere along the line, the quagmire in his head had turned into a stream of liquid fire.

Although he wasn't sure the voice that emerged was his, the words certainly were. "Love you right back, Doc. Have from the moment I met you, formaldehyde notwithstanding."

He knew she lowered her mouth to his. He could feel her breath on his skin. He smiled when a very different kind of fire ignited in his lower body. Had to be a good sign, right?

"I thought you might be awake," she said and kissed him.

"Am I?" His mind began to slip away. Thankfully, though, not back into the abyss, only into sleep. "Wake me," he murmured, "when the killer ants crawling around in my chest move out."

"It's a promise," she said and kissed him again. "Sleep well, Lieutenant. You've got a lot to come back to. I wish I could say all of it was good…."

"YOU SURE YOU WANT TO DO this, Tal?" The medical examiner set a hand on the sheet that covered McVey's body.

Tal let his lips quirk. "Been talking to Cassie Styles, huh?"

"You know how word travels."

"Yeah, I know. Do it, Gord."

The man drew the sheet back, glanced over, then made a discreet exit.

Tal stared. He couldn't do much else at this point. His mind was still fogged from a battery of painkillers. Not so many, though, that he missed the resemblance.

Hadn't he noticed it before? Denied it?

He'd called himself McVey. He'd been coming to this hospital since Maya was a resident. He'd known her almost as long as Tal had. He'd been a semi-regular patient. He'd gone to her and only her for treatment. He'd borrowed a dead man's identity to sustain the facade. He'd kept his distance from the police. He'd made a point of that, Tal realized. He'd watched but never approached. He hadn't intruded, hadn't disrupted.

He'd saved Maya's life.

Perching on a high stool, Tal continued to stare. And for the first time since childhood, he let the memories come.

MAYA OPTED FOR A LONG shower in the doctors' lounge. It gave Tal time to do what she knew he needed to do. Confront a ghost from his past. Hopefully exorcise it. At least come to terms with it.

He was waiting in the lounge when she returned from the shower bathroom, towel-drying her hair.

He motioned to a box on the floor. "Anything interesting?"

"Just stuff." She studied his face. "You're pale."

"Everyone's pale under fluorescents. Is that a leather jacket?"

"Tal, you said Adam's brother could have it. Believe me, you wouldn't like anything in there, not the music, not the movies and definitely not the torn jacket."

"Definitely not." He smiled a little. "Drake called. He ate some bad pork after Perine's aborted party."

"I heard. Ptomaine. Very uncomfortable. He won't be his usual bouncy self for several days."

"Sellers had the eight-tracks from the car examined. They really were Abba tapes. Nothing information-wise inside."

Her eyes danced. "There's no accounting for taste, huh?"

"I don't hate Abba, Maya."

When he leaned his good shoulder on a cabinet, she strolled over, blew at his hair. "You're sexy when you're wounded, Lieutenant."

"Painkillers are wearing off."

"Want more?"

Trapping her chin between his fingers and thumb, he kissed her long and deep. "Not a chance. I want to feel. I need to. Nate wasn't the man I thought he was. That hurts like hell. Probably always will."

She stroked his cheek. "What got you looking in his direction? I mean the first thing."

Tal's gaze traveled to an indistinct point on the wall. "I'm not sure. It started with a gut feeling, a twinge, nothing more than that. I ignored it. It came back. Something about him had changed over the past few years. I felt it, couldn't explain it. Wasn't sure I wanted to."

"Did you suspect him of killing Adam?"

"Part of me did. It wasn't quite Perine's style. Close, but a little off."

"Do you think Perine's ever killed anyone?"

"Yeah, I think he has. Can I prove it? Not right now."

"Tal, please say you're not going to become obsessed with catching him."

"I'm not an obsessive person." He glanced away, allowed a trace of amusement through. "Not sure how McGraw will react, though."

The fingers that had been playing with his hair stopped. "And McGraw's reaction matters because?"

"He's been transferred to homicide."

Oddly enough, Maya didn't dislike that scenario. "Reward for saving your life?"

Tal's smile was faint. "You did that, Maya. McGraw took a bullet. Nate knocked me down, but you'd already escaped. He had no choice. He had to pursue."

"He told me he was dying," she said. "Hinted at it really, but I believed him. I wanted to tell you. I just wasn't sure how."

"Keep 'em off balance. It was one of his mottoes. Get people looking in one direction so you can ambush them from another."

"That's an old magician's trick."

"Think of him as an old magician."

"What sealed the deal for you?"

"His house was wrong. You know that part. It was the red thermos that did it. I was in an alley with McGraw, and I saw a broken red thermos lying next to a garbage bag. That's when my mind flashed a picture of another red thermos I'd seen."

"At Perine's party?" She smiled at his narrowed eyes. "I saw it, too. In an old man's lap, right? He was in a wheelchair. His blanket slipped, but not before I spotted the red thermos. It was exactly like the one Nate carried. Okay, maybe Nate had disguised himself so he could sneak past Perine, but why keep that a secret from you, from us, from anyone involved except Perine?"

"Excellent cop question, Maya."

"Thank you. Here's another. If Nate knew who Falcon was, why did he come to the party? Unless…" A new thought struck. "Did he suspect Falcon would show?"

"Probably. And who knew? Maybe Nate could've cornered him. What he didn't want was for us to corner him."

"Which is why he plowed into McGraw's leg." She bit her lip. "Do you know if Nate had a room at the hotel for the night? I saw the old man he'd become drop a key. When I couldn't catch his eye, I turned it in to the front desk. It was a room key. Six-one-seven."

"Opie Frame," Tal replied.

"Excuse me?"

"That's the name he used to register. Yes, he took a room. O. P. Frame, Maya, or more aptly, Frame O. P., which was his goal from the start—to frame Orlando Perine. Nate enjoyed a healthy dose of irony. I guess he couldn't resist at that point."

"Figured that one out alone, huh, Lieutenant?"

"Hey, cell phone, time on my hands, loose ends to tie."

"So how's Drake with all this?"

"He'll survive. He worked with Nate, but they were never close." Tal let his forehead drop onto hers. "This is gonna hurt for a long, long time."

"I know." Taking his face in her hands, she looked into his eyes. "You'll get through it, Tal. All of it. I'll help you get through it."

The barest hint of a smile crossed his lips. "Is that a clever segue to McVey?"

She trod carefully. "Are you okay knowing he was your father?"

"Let's say I'm reevaluating some of my less positive beliefs."

"He, uh…hmm. Actually, I'm not sure what to say. I told you he seemed familiar to me. Must have been because of you." She pressed her palms to his chest. "Right before he died, he admitted he was a bad husband and a worse father. He wanted me to tell you he was sorry. He wanted you to be happy and to know that he wished he could have been there for you. He wanted me to tell you goodbye."

Tal glanced away, then back. "I want to feel something for him, Maya, but I don't. I can't. Not yet."

"You will," she promised, "in time. He wasn't the monster you thought he was, whereas Nate, well, Nate was. That's a lot for anyone, cop or civilian, to take in."

"It's a lot for ten cops or civilians to take in. Like I said, it'll take time."

"And that temper you were so worried about?"

"Under control. I realized downstairs that I could never hurt you, Dr. S. Couldn't even entertain the possibility." He skimmed his thumb over the nick at her temple. "And speaking of…"

"It's nothing. A scratch." She gave his wrist a playful kiss. "I knocked heads with Cassie when you launched us into the wall. That was you, right, and not McGraw?"

"It was me. McGraw wasn't supposed to be there. He blindsided me before I got to you. I told him to go for backup. Guess he decided he was backup enough. In any case, we'll be riding together for a few months."

A disbelieving laugh bubbled up. "You and Mc-Graw?"

"Call it another of life's many twists. Personally, I call it a test. If I don't kill him, I'll know I can handle anything."

"As I've said all along." Sliding her hands very carefully to his shoulders, she moved temptingly closer. "So is that it, then? Are we done? Case closed, and we can fly to wherever for a nice, long vacation?"

"Or fly to wherever and get married."

"Okay, now you're talking bombshell. I'm just getting my head around the 'I'm in love with you and you're in love with me' thing."

"Old news, Maya. It's time to move forward."

"Moving forward," she agreed and gave her hips a teasing roll.

"Excuse me, Dr. Santino? Oh." Her cheeks flaming, Cassie froze in the doorway. "Sorry. Really sorry. It's just that some CDs dropped out of the box the officer brought in for you. I'm, uh, glad you're better, Lieutenant. I—Here." She thrust the disks at Maya and backed out.

"She's recovering." As Maya started to drop the CDs into the box, she spied one of the titles and did an amused double take. "Oh, look, *Dead Wallflowers II*. Wanna listen?"

"To 'The Death March' on electric guitar? I'll pass."

"Coward," she accused. "You could try it, if only for Adam's…" She trailed off, as the title of the download underneath leaped out at her. "Great White Sharks?"

"Sounds vicious."

"Doesn't it?" She turned the case toward him. "The Great White Sharks, Tal, whose CD just happens to be called *Life in a Goldfish Bowl*."

His eyes narrowed on the title. Taking the disk from her hand, he allowed a slow smile to appear. "That's one big fish," he agreed.

"Isn't it? In a very small pond." A canny brow went up. "Possible the case might be fully wrapped up now, Lieutenant?"

"In terms of Falcon's information, maybe. In terms of you, I've been fully wrapped up for seven years."

Catching one of the belt loops on his jeans, Maya tugged him gently toward her. "Time to blow the sharks and all of your misconceptions out of the water, Tal. You're an excellent cop and an even better man."

"I still have to look into McVey's…"

"Lieutenant?"

"What?"

"Forget McVey. Forget your mother and Nate and everyone not in this room right now. You said I've had you wrapped up for seven years." She tugged again until their mouths were less than an inch apart. "I want to start unwrapping."

✦ ✦ ✦ ✦ ✦

In honor of our 60th anniversary,
Harlequin® American Romance® is celebrating by
featuring an all-American male each month,
all year long with
MEN MADE IN AMERICA!
This June, we'll be featuring American men
living in the West.

Here's a sneak preview of
THE CHIEF RANGER by Rebecca Winters.

Chief Ranger Vance Rossiter has to confront the sister
of a man who died while under Vance's watch...and
also confront his attraction to her.

"Chief Ranger Rossiter?" The sight of the woman who'd stepped inside Vance's office brought him to his feet. "I'm Rachel Darrow. Your secretary said I should come right in."

"Please," he said, walking around his desk to shake her hand. At a glance he estimated she was in her mid-twenties. Her feminine curves did wonders for the pale blue T-shirt and jeans she was wearing. "Ranger Jarvis informed me there's a young boy with you."

The unfriendly expression in her beautiful green eyes caught him off guard. "Yes," was her clipped reply. "When we arrived in Yosemite the ranger told me I couldn't go anywhere in the park until I talked to you first."

"That's right."

"Knowing you wanted this meeting to be private, he offered to show my nephew around Headquarters."

So this woman was the victim's sister…. "What's his name?"

"Nicky."

The boy who haunted Vance's dreams now had a name. "How old is he?"

"He turned six three weeks ago. Were you the man in charge when my brother and sister-in-law were killed?"

"Yes. To tell you I'm sorry for what happened couldn't begin to convey my feelings."

The woman's gaze didn't flicker. "I won't even try to describe mine. Just tell me one thing. Was their accident preventable?"

"Yes," he answered without hesitation.

"In other words, the people working under you fell asleep on your watch and two lives were snuffed out as a result."

Hearing it put like that, he had to set the record straight. "My staff had nothing to do with it. I, myself, could have prevented the loss of life."

Ms. Darrow's expression hardened. "So you admit culpability."

"Yes. I take full blame."

A look of pain crossed over her features. "You can just stand there and admit it?" Her cry echoed that of his own tortured soul.

"Yes." He sucked in his breath.

"I work for a cruise line. Aboard ship, it's the captain's responsibility to maintain rigid safety regulations. If a disaster like that had happened while he was in charge he would have been relieved of his command and never given another ship again."

Rachel Darrow couldn't know she was preaching to the converted. "If you've come to the park with the intention of bringing a lawsuit against me for negligence, maybe you should." It would only be what he deserved.

"Maybe I will."

In the next instant, she wheeled around and hurried out of his office. Vance could have gone after her, but it would cause a scene, something he was loath to do for a variety of reasons. In the first place, he needed to cool down before he approached her again.

The discovery of the Darrows' frozen bodies had affected every ranger in the park. A little boy had been orphaned—a boy whose aunt was all he had left.

⁎ ⁎ ⁎ ⁎ ⁎

Will Rachel allow Vance to explain—and will she let him into her heart?
Find out in
THE CHIEF RANGER.
Available June 2009 from Harlequin® American Romance®.

We'll be spotlighting a different series every month
throughout 2009 to celebrate our 60th anniversary.

Look for Harlequin®
American Romance® in June!

Join us for a year-long celebration of the rugged
American male! From cops to cowboys—
Men Made in America has the hero
you've been dreaming about!

Look for

The Chief Ranger

by Rebecca Winters, on sale in June!

Escape Around the World

Dream destinations, whirlwind weddings!

Honeymoon with the Boss
by
JESSICA HART

Top tycoon Tom Maddison is used to calling the
shots—until his convenient marriage falls through.
But rather than waste his honeymoon, he'll take
his boardroom to the beach and bring his oh-so-
sensible secretary Imogen on a tropical business
trip! But will Tom finally see the sexy woman
that prudent Imogen truly is?

Available in June wherever books are sold.

REQUEST YOUR FREE BOOKS!

2 FREE NOVELS PLUS 2 FREE GIFTS!

◆ HARLEQUIN®
INTRIGUE®

Breathtaking Romantic Suspense

YES! Please send me 2 FREE Harlequin Intrigue® novels and my 2 FREE gifts (gifts are worth about $10). After receiving them, if I don't wish to receive any more books, I can return the shipping statement marked "cancel." If I don't cancel, I will receive 6 brand-new novels every month and be billed just $4.24 per book in the U.S. or $4.99 per book in Canada. That's a savings of close to 15% off the cover price! It's quite a bargain! Shipping and handling is just 50¢ per book.* I understand that accepting the 2 free books and gifts places me under no obligation to buy anything. I can always return a shipment and cancel at any time. Even if I never buy another book from Harlequin, the two free books and gifts are mine to keep forever.

182 HDN EYTR   382 HDN EYT3

Name	(PLEASE PRINT)

Address	Apt. #

City	State/Prov.	Zip/Postal Code

Signature (if under 18, a parent or guardian must sign)

Mail to the **Harlequin Reader Service:**
IN U.S.A.: P.O. Box 1867, Buffalo, NY 14240-1867
IN CANADA: P.O. Box 609, Fort Erie, Ontario L2A 5X3

Not valid to current subscribers of Harlequin Intrigue books.

**Are you a current subscriber of Harlequin Intrigue books
and want to receive the larger-print edition?
Call 1-800-873-8635 today!**

* Terms and prices subject to change without notice. Prices do not include applicable taxes. Sales tax applicable in N.Y. Canadian residents will be charged applicable provincial taxes and GST. Offer not valid in Quebec. This offer is limited to one order per household. All orders subject to approval. Credit or debit balances in a customer's account(s) may be offset by any other outstanding balance owed by or to the customer. Please allow 4 to 6 weeks for delivery. Offer available while quantities last.

Your Privacy: Harlequin is committed to protecting your privacy. Our Privacy Policy is available online at www.eHarlequin.com or upon request from the Reader Service. From time to time we make our lists of customers available to reputable third parties who may have a product or service of interest to you. If you would prefer we not share your name and address, please check here. ☐

HI09R

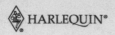

INTRIGUE®

COMING NEXT MONTH

Available June 9, 2009

#1137 BIG SKY DYNASTY by B.J. Daniels

Whitehorse, Montana: The Corbetts

The hunky ranch owner believes his deranged ex-wife is dead—until he finds out she has returned to town and wormed her way into the life of a sweet and trusting knit shop owner. He's ready to risk his life to save them both from a dangerous obsession.

#1138 PULLING THE TRIGGER by Julie Miller

Kenner County Crime Unit

A suspected murderer has escaped into the mountains, but two of Kenner County's finest are hot on his trail. The only thing hotter is the attraction that still sizzles between these former lovers. Can they catch their man and resurrect their love?

#1139 MIDNIGHT INVESTIGATION by Sheryl Lynn

The feisty skeptic is unimpressed by the tall, well-built police officer who claims psychic abilities—until she unknowingly invites a malevolent spirit home. Now the man she doubted may be the only one who can help….

#1140 HEIRESS RECON by Carla Cassidy

The Recovery Men

The former-navy SEAL is in the business of recovery, but he never figured his job would call for repossessing a beautiful heiress. He has promised her father that he will keep her safe from the threats that are being made against her life, but can he guard his heart as well?

#1141 THE PHANTOM OF BLACK'S COVE by Jan Hambright

He's a Mystery

The isolated clinic in Black's Cove holds many secrets, and the investigative journalist is ready to uncover all—until the owner's grandson tries to stop her. Can these secrets be dangerous enough to endanger both of their lives?

#1142 ROYAL PROTOCOL by Dana Marton

Defending the Crown

When the opera house he designed is overtaken by rebels, the prince stays behind to protect his masterpiece—and the beautiful young diva that is trapped with him. Surviving opening night takes on a whole new meaning as they fight for their lives.

www.eHarlequin.com